I0640050

John Alfred Langford

**Shelley**

The death of St. Polycarp, and other poems

John Alfred Langford

**Shelley**
*The death of St. Polycarp, and other poems*

ISBN/EAN: 9783337388249

Printed in Europe, USA, Canada, Australia, Japan

Cover: Foto ©Andreas Hilbeck / pixelio.de

More available books at **www.hansebooks.com**

# SHELLEY:

## THE DEATH OF ST. POLYCARP,

AND

## Other Poems.

BY JOHN ALFRED LANGFORD,

AUTHOR OF

"THE LAMP OF LIFE," "POEMS OF THE FIELDS AND TOWN,"

ETC. ETC.

LONDON:

SMITH, ELDER AND CO., 65, CORNHILL.

———

M.DCCC.LX.

TO

# SIR PERCY FLORENCE

AND THE

# HON. LADY JANE SHELLEY,

THE FOLLOWING TRIBUTE TO THE MEMORY OF

# THE IMMORTAL POET,

WHOSE NAME THEY INHERIT,

IS RESPECTFULLY INSCRIBED BY

THE AUTHOR.

# CONTENTS.

# SHELLEY.

"He had a gentle yet aspiring mind ;
    Just, innocent, with varied learning fed,
And such as glorious consolation find
    In others' joy, when all their own is dead :
He lived, and laboured for his kind in grief,
    And yet, unlike all others, it is said,
That from such toil he never found relief.
    Although a child of fortune and of power,
Of an ancestral name the orphan chief,
    His soul had wedded wisdom, and her dower
Is love and justice."         PRINCE ATHANASE.

---

"Our toil from thought all glorious forms shall cull,
To make this Earth, our home, more beautiful,
And Science, and her sister Poesy,
Shall clothe in light the fields and cities of the free!"
        THE REVOLT OF ISLAM.

---

"In love, and beauty, and delight,
    There is no death nor change ; their might
        Exceeds our organs, which endure
        No light, being themselves obscure."
        THE SENSITIVE PLANT.

# SHELLEY.

MAN's noblest labour is to war with wrong;

Against oppression to uplift his voice;

To shield the weak from the assailing strong;

To make the sorrow-stricken heart rejoice;

To bless the virtuous seeking virtue's choice

In evil times; the patriot aid to lend,

Despite of tyrant might, or rabble noise;

To raise the low, the wretched to defend;

The world, and the world's ways, in hopefulness to mend.

## 2.

The task is hard.   For life is full of care :
Success is sovereign over all ; and men
In triumph will the gilded evil bear,
And strew the crowded way with flowers; and when
Poor, patient merit seeks to rise again,
Scorn meets his ears, and thorns his path bestrew,
And darkness hems him round ; full in his ken
The thistle beds are placed, and he may view
The Despond Slough men make for him to travel through.

## 3.

Yet earth was viler when my hero bore
The day-by-day-increasing burden—life.
But over all the ills his mind did soar,
And bravely met, and grappled with the strife
Which bowed his heart with sorrow; for the knife
Smote keenly, and he suffered while he fought ;
And wept in secret, seeing pain so rife.
For woe succeeded woe, as each one caught
At some delusive hope, or dark despairing thought.

## 4.

His young mind, nurtured mid all lovely things,
Had caught their beauty and their loveliness :
And sanguine as the joy which first love flings
Around her, through life's wrongs he strove to press ;
And blest himself the suffering he would bless ;
Would ease the aching heart and stay the tear ;
The anguish and its cause alike suppress ;
Make smiling lips, and joyous fronts appear,
Where forehead-lining grief its sad abode would rear.

## 5.

He loved the whole creation.   Unto him
The grass, the flower, the tree, had each a tongue,
And ever in his presence used to hymn
Sweet themes of joy.   And musically strong,
All chorusing of love, arose the song
Of birds ; to him the ever-murmuring streams ;
The gilded insects in their buzzing throng ;
The winds that soothe you into pleasant dreams,
And every voice of nature sung the same sweet themes.

## 6.

The ocean was his teacher ; and the sky,

With its continuous changefulness of glory,

Filled his young soul with aspirations high.

The mountains, heather-clad, or wild and hoary,

Found food for him in their bewitching story

Of ages past : he from their summits saw

The golden-glebèd plain, or promontory

That wantoned with the sea : and thence would draw

Deep strength, and pure resolve to war 'gainst tyrant law.


## 7.

In nature's glorious workings he beheld

The wondrous harmony of laws divine ;

Their beauty and their peace his spirit held

As with enchantment : at her flower-strewn shrine,

He, day and night, a worshipper, would twine

His highest hopes into a wreath of song,

And woo her with sweet music to combine

Her love with his : his love was pure and strong,

And nature smiled her " Yes," and did to him belong.

### 8.

He loved her with the passionate devotion
Of one who her divineness feels and sees.
Her presence thrilled him with intense emotion.
The soaring slave, whom Death from fetters frees,
His spirit wand'ring over freedom's seas,
Has for his pale deliverer scarce the love,
Which filled his heart at sight of fields and trees.
The visible universe, around, above,
To unimaginable bliss could all his senses move.

### 9.

And of her beauty and her freedom, he
The spirit caught.   They lit in him the fire
Which will not die ; will never quenched be ;
But once illumed keeps soaring high and higher,
A thing of love, immortal as its sire.
A child of heaven,—whatever tempests blow
It burns, and burns, and burning will aspire,
Until its brightness beams on all below,
And earth is glorified for aye with her intensest glow.

## 10.

And loved and loving thus he grew in years,
The child of Hope and Hope-fed Liberty;
His heart untouched by any earthly fears,
With lion courage, lamb-like mildness he
Was richly dowered; and bravely dared to be
All that his nature was.   As thought to thought,
He answered to each generous impulse, free,
And bared his heart with holiest yearnings fraught;
To bless his fellow men the sole reward he sought.

## 11.

And from the varied annals of the past,
The records of the wise, the free, and good;
Of men whose high, heroic acts had cast
A splendour round the age in which they stood,
In stedfast, self-denying fortitude,
The scorn, the anguish, and the pain to bear,
And seal a noble cause with noble blood—
His mind he stored with such examples fair,
And fortified his soul to suffer and to dare.

## 12.

And instruments of torture thus became
The holy relics of a former time ;
The signs of tyrants' impotence and shame,
The symbols of the vanity of crime,
And the eternity of love sublime ;
To which the after generations turn
To gather strength and wisdom, as from slime
The serpent wins its beauty ; whence men learn
How for a great and self-absorbing cause to burn.

## 13.

Th' heroic deeds of Greek and Roman story ;
Of willing 'death to guard their country's name ;
Of sacrifice for freedom's sunny glory ;
Of love, of nobleness, resolve, and fame ;
Of hearts that scorned all meanness, and became
A fire of indignation to behold,
The weak oppressed ; and flashed in outward flame
At tyranny and wrong : all this was gold
Of virgin worth to him, whose price could not be told.

### 14.

And in the golden realms of poesy
A free-born citizen, he journeyed on ;
His path lit by the light which none may see
But souls of purest love ; and there he won
A glorious rule, and bright dominion.
A crown of fragrant amaranthine flowers,
That o'er his flowing hair as sunbeams shone ;
And in his open heart rained music's showers,
And all his being filled with song's imperial powers.

### 15.

Each nation strung for him her own sweet lyre,
And every poet smiled upon his love.
In every vein he felt the glowing fire
Of exquisite delight which made him prove
The littleness of things, which most men move
To action ; and his spirit fondly dwelt
On thoughts which raise the seeking mind above
All low desires ; he lived in song, and felt
The ecstacy of those who at such shrines have knelt.

## 16.

And wooing thus the beautiful and fair,

As pure as love, as strong as hope he grew.

And noble thoughts came to him unaware

As part of his own nature ; did imbue

Him with the martyr spirit through and through,

And faith in virtue's triumph ; in the great

And deathless victory of the good and true,

Bright visions of a future did create

Of Love, and Truth, and Mercy ruling every state.


## 17.

But oh, the shock, the pang, the agony,

Which tore his very being when he turned

From Nature's ever-glorious empiry,

And from the world of song, where is inurned

The might and splendour of the past ; he burned

With fiery wrath at all he there beheld.

How dark compared with that for which he yearned !

There tyranny a black dominion held,

And wrong was lord below, and might all strivings quelled.

### 18.

The seat, miscalled of Justice, was unjust ;
The blood-stained instrument of shameless might ;
The poor man's scourge : eat up with lies and rust
From darker times, obscuring truth and right.
Blind but to poverty, and worth, and light ;
And eager with the sword to quench in blood
The fire of godlike hopes ; the fatal blight
Of freedom ; terror of the wise and good ;
And stern oppressor of the toiling multitude.


### 19.

And in the Church was bigotry and hate ;
The priest, enslaved by superstition's power,
Profaned the office of God's delegate,
And sold himself for gold ; forgot his dower
Of blessedness and love ; shook from the flower
Of Christian Mercy all its rich perfume,
And made man's lovers curse the fatal hour
That bright religion clothed herself in gloom,
And turned a gracious God into the Lord of doom.

## 20.

For round His very altars gathered then
The enemies of knowledge, love, and grace.
And crime and wrong were sanctified by men
Sworn to uphold the right ; to keep a place
For suffering weakness ; to afford solace
To wretchedness howe'er produced : but they
With power had made a union, and disgrace,
Hypocrisy, and fraud, and lies held sway,
Where bright-eyed truth with mild-eyed innocence should
    play.

## 21.

The throne had its high functions laid aside,
And was no more the seat of righteousness ;
But arrogance, and isolating pride,
And beggar-making grandeur, with the press
Of palace-haunting slaves of greediness,
And freedom-hating sycophants held rule,
And laughed and fattened on the land's distress.
The wise man's place was guarded by the fool ;
And honest toil bowed down into the lordling's tool.

### 22.

The Church, the Palace, and the Halls of law,
Perverted from their noble ends, had grown
Like vultures fattening an unholy maw
Upon corruption ; far and wide was thrown
Their baleful influence ; the sigh, the groan,
The silent tear that furrowed misery's face,
The famine-stricken cheek, the dying moan
Of free men fettered by their bondage base,—
By these, and kindred signs their being men might trace.

### 23.

And if such wrongs e'er found a pleading voice—
As spite of danger brave men will arise—
That made of the ignoble cause its choice,
To rend the veil of pomp, and show the lies
Which filled the state ; how by the agonies
Of thousands was the ermined splendour bought ;
The air rung with the loud assailing cries
Of traitor, atheist, madman, zealot fraught
With every devilish sin by which perdition's caught.

## 24.

'Twas so with him.  His sanguine heart, inspired

With all that makes men generous and free,—

By hope, by love, and bright impulses fired,

To bless the world with heavenly liberty,

With holy joy, and social harmony,

When free from hate, from care, from woe, and strife,

Bound in fraternal bonds mankind should be ;

And every heart, and every homestead rife

With tenderness, and grace, and all that blesses life.


## 25.

For this' he gave up wealth, and ease, and fame,

And threw himself into the battle's van,

Regardless of the scoffs, the jeers, the shame,

The Church's execration, and the ban

Of all who in the common courses ran ;

Such things he heeded not, but for the right

He laboured on ; and followed still the plan

His heart approved ; and there with all his might

He bore himself as fits a hero in the fight.

### 26.

He saw the worst of wrongs and ills were done,
Or being done; were by the Church approved;
That she held with the strong; her foot was on
The bended neck of poverty, nor moved
But at the bidding of the Power she loved.
For then Religion's high and holy name
Was draggled in the mire, and proved
What unimaginable depths of shame
The noblest things can bear when lies have sapped their
    fame.

### 27.

Beside oppression's throne he saw the priest:
He heard him bless the sword's unholy might;
And sanctify the law which pierced the breast
Of Justice and of Mercy: vaunt the right
Of kings to be their people's scourge and blight:
Defend the crimes of hoar antiquity;
And curse the men who sought to see the light,
To raise the toilers from their misery,
And bid the Church-and-king-oppressed slaves be free.

## 28.

God's sacred name, and Christ's divinest life,

He saw in all the temples were profaned—

The place of love changed to the seat of strife;

Injustice at the altar steps maintained

As God's appointed law; corruption-stained

And crime-ensanguined deeds receive the praise

Of men miscalled His servants; who sustained

The reign of darkness, hiding still the rays

Of truth, and love, and light, in superstition's maze.


## 29.

And all with hearts to feel, and eyes to see

The wrong, the shame, the anguish and the woe,

Which men endured from such iniquity,

And dared the sin-concealing veil to throw

Aside, that all the dreadful truth might know,

Were by these surpliced lords in wrath denounced

. Blasphemers of the Holy One below ;

And prisons here, hereafter hell, pronounced

The fit abodes of those who nobler times announced.

### 30.

Thus in Religion's name were evils done,
And round such crimes Religion's veil was thrown:
Whatever lawless Might resolved upon
The Church with willing speed declared her own:
And vain the people's prayer, the people's groan,
Or deep unuttered curse ; for thus combined,
The powers of darkness ruled supreme, alone—
An angel looking down had not divined
That England then called Christ the Prince of all mankind.

### 31.

And he, unselfish, loving, young, and bold,
Before the down had graced his youthful chin,
Before a line upon his face had told
Of cares without, or sufferings within ;
His soul entranced, his heart untouched by sin,
With divine pity only moved and swayed,
Resolved the praises of the good to win,
And dare the worst to crush the idol made
By selfishness and sin, and custom's iron trade.

### 32.

And like young David, from a rippling brook,
Whose waters were to him a sweet delight,
A little, smooth, and blue-veined pebble took,
And slung it 'gainst Goliath in his might ;
And, though the stone rebounded, hit him right
Upon the forehead ; making such a wound,
That never since the giant's tongue could bite
With half its venom ; never since has found
Such willing slaves to grovel when in rage he frowned.


### 33.

But woe to him who struck the fatal blow !
The many whom with blessing he would bless,
Shrank back affrighted ; for they did not know
Bright freedom's voice ; so long had wretchedness.
And wrong, and bondage, and the soul's distress,
Their nobler feelings slain.   Not so the few
Who revelled in the dearth of nobleness,
And clad in Pharisaic robes, withdrew
Beyond the sound of plaints their own misdoings drew.

### 34.

Like bloodhounds swift they rushed upon their prey,
And hurled their thunderbolts upon his head :
" Anathema," was all their lips could say ;
And this in many forms they freely spread.
They banned him from the seat where knowledge fed
The aspirations of his yearning soul ;
Where oft the muses had their darling led
Was he to walk no more ; nor for him roll
The spirit-haunted Isis, rich in glory's scroll.

### 35.

Oh, mourn for one so young, so great, and good !
Oh, mourn the want of human charity !
Oh, mourn the weakness of the multitude !
And mourn that power should harsh and cruel be !
Was there no heart with purity to see
The deep and holy love that fired his tongue ?
No hand to guide ? no magnanimity
Which from the depths of its own fountain strong,
Could shield and honour him so valiant and so young ?

## 36.

Not one.   Away, away to banishment,

Cast branded on the world; marked worse than Cain.

Among his cruel fellows he was sent

To dare the battle, and to bear the pain—

A brand for burning, a victim to be slain.

What matter he was mild, and good, and kind:

Had love and charity that would sustain

A world of woe to save the merest hind

From misery and wrong : to virtue they were blind.


## 37.

And he who should have shielded, counselled, led

The young heart to its fitting resting-place,

With fiery wrath his malediction shed,

And banished him from hearth, and home, and grace,

As alien to, a blot upon, his race.

Thus sorrow came on sorrow, woe on woe ;

And he was wounded in the tenderest place,

His home affections, by that cruel blow,

And from his bleeding heart a flood of grief did flow.

### 38.

Alone, alone, with none to cheer or bless,
An exile in his native land he lived.
And with his fragile frame, his tenderness,
And heart that yearned for love, how he survived
The storm that hate, and zeal, and power unhived,
Had poured on him, none, save himself, may tell.
He bore the burden bravely; and revived
By kindly deeds the hopes which fondly dwell
On holier, happier times when hearts with love shall swell.


### 39.

A few still watched him with a tender care,
His mother's changeless love was his to prize,
And gentle maidens wove a garland fair
Of sisterly affection, to surprise
And soothe him in his lonely life.   As lies
Upon the bosom of an ebon night,
One bright and only star, and each one cries,
How beautiful! so shone amidst the blight
Of his dark, restless lot, these blessed rays of light.

### 40.

And thus he went, a sad and stricken deer,

To mingle with the cold, unheeding herd:

But none his bright eye saw dimmed by a tear,

Or from his lips complaining murmurs heard.

He breathed no curse; forgiveness was the word,

And sorrow for the wrongs he could not cure.

He mourned in secret; and his soul was stirred

E'en to its depths to see mankind endure

Continually to drink from fountains so impure.


### 41.

Unto his Mother Nature he returned,

And threw himself upon her loving breast:

And she, with heart that for her darling yearned,

In her wide arms enfolded him, imprest

Her warmest kisses on his lips; carest

Him in a thousand mild, endearing ways;

With richest balsam, and pure ointments prest

From out her sweetest flowers, his hurt she stays;

And for her favourite one her brightest smiles displays.

### 42.

Her hills, her woods, her rivers were the scenes
In which he worshipped her; in solitudes,
In forest dells, wild heaths, and dark ravines,
By waterfalls, and raging torrent floods,
Secluded spots where rarely man intrudes,
He found the peace and joy which solace pain,
And bring the thoughts on which the fancy broods,
Till ecstacy possesses heart and brain,
And overflows the soul like gentle Summer rain.

### 43.

With beauty and with grandeur day and night,
He held deep intercourse; and from them drew
Their many meanings, teachings infinite.
So strong his love, so well he learned to woo,
At length their deeper mysteries he knew;
Their language understood; and won the power
To pierce their mystic-woven curtain through;
Their glorious splendours on the world to shower;—
And thus he lived with song and suffering for his dower.

### 44.

With all the varying forms of loveliness ;
With all the aspects of sublimity ;
With all the sounds of sweet deliciousness ;
With Nature bound in Summer trance, or free
In Winter's elemental strife, was he
Familiar ; and he loved her smiles and tears ;
In all her changeful shapes and graces she
Was dear to him.   His deep love banished fears,
And stronger grew his trust as passed the mournful years.

### 45.

And pillowed on one arm he oft would lie
For hours upon the grassed and flowery ground,
And gaze entranced into the silent sky,
Whose poet-coloured splendours flitting round
With wondrous visions, held his fancy bound.
And fairy forms ethereal and bright,
In realms of golden glory there he found,
Who told to him their lives of love and light,
Which he resang to men in strains of sweet delight.

### 46.

Adown a river's rich and varied course,
Would he, a solitary, idly float ;
Pure inspirations gathering from the source
Whence inspirations come, while o'er his boat
The water-kissing foliage hung ; and note
On note from every music-dowered bird,
Would thrill him with its lay, and from his throat
Invisible, the lark his rapture stirred,
Till he the song received ;—resang it word for word.

### 47.

The spirits which the woods and streams enshrine ;
The dwellers in the grass, the trees, the flowers ;
The presences which make all things divine ;
The midday, and the midnight haunting powers ;
The graces which attend the fleeting hours ;
The beings that unseen, still people space,
And bring their blessings with the sun and showers,
With him held converse, and for him would trace
The ever-present glories of their dwelling-place.

### 48.

And in this poet-world he lived alone ;
And with its bright inhabitants he dwelt,
Till life became a portion of their own,
And all their feelings into his did melt.
Their spiritual existences were felt
As pure realities ; and thus became
The subjects of his song, which boldly reft
The grace, the power, the sweetness, and the flame
Of the bright interlunar world from which they came.


### 49.

In strains harmonious as ever fell
From lips of poet in divinest hours,
Did he the wondrous revelations tell
Of mystic kingdoms and of mystic powers ;
Mind's noblest workings, and the thought which dowers
Man's life with glory, beauty, and with awe ;
The love which cheers ; the joys which are its flowers ;
The sorrows that oppress ; the truths that draw
His judgment first to know, then gladly bow to law.

## 50.

The pain, the triumph, and the ecstacy ;
The grandeur and the mystery of life ;
The loveliness and the sublimity
Of all the visible universe, whose strife
Is desolation, and whose peace is rife
With all that can entrance with visions bright ;
Of Liberty, with Love, his wedded wife,
Together leading man through darkest night
To uplands of sweet peace, and homes of calm delight.

## 51.

Such were his themes ; as glorious as e'er
The heart of man with prophecy inspired.
The poets are our prophets.  He, the seer,
By love's absorbing soul possessed, and fired
By all the truth and beauty he admired,
The world with purer, truer life to bless:
For this he toiled, and from man's paths retired,
And shunned the noise, the tumult, and the press,
That he might purify his heart in loneliness.

## 52.

And sorrow was his lot.   The martyr fate
He with the martyr-spirit had received ;
He blessed, was cursed ; his love was met with hate ;
And few there were that for his sufferings grieved ;
And fewer still those sufferings e'er relieved.
Love that brings joy to all, to him brought woe ;
Its smiles for him in tears had been conceived ;
Death held the wedding veil ; and soon the blow,
O'erwhelming sense and thought, came from the biding foe.

## 53.

The heavenly ties of parent and of child ;
All that is meant when " Father" lisping falls
From infant lips, so pure and undefiled ;
The hopes which gather round that name ; the calls
For tenderness ; the sport which never palls
When children are our playfellows ; the sound
Of sunny laughter ringing through the halls
Of happy homes ; all these he might have found :
But man profaned his hearth, law blasted while it bound.

## 54.

While still a father, he was childless made
By power that heeded not the sense of right ;
That dared domestic sacredness invade ;
Scorned Nature's pleading voice, with shameful might
Sought wedded love's serenest flowers to blight ;
And in Religion's holy name profaned
The cause Religion should with chief delight
Surround with all its awe, and keep unstained
From sacrilegious touch of wrong by might maintained.

## 55.

Life's purest pleasures were to him denied,
Or, mixed with gall and wormwood, brought him pain.
Chivalrous kindness bound him to a bride
Love crowned not with his blessing ; weak and vain
It is to struggle 'gainst love's binding rein ;
And so he found it.   There was grief, and woe,
And desolation in his heart's domain ;
And death in hideous form did round him throw
Its dread and direful shadow, weird and wild, I trow.

## 56.

That shadow hung around him for a time,
And tracked his footsteps with its fearful gloom,
And haunted like the ghost of some great crime
That makes itself its punishment and doom:
Impalpable, but potent to consume
Whate'er of peace, whate'er of joy remains,
Till life all darkness is ; no rays illume
Its dark ravines, its wild and arid plains ;
But anguish uncontrolled o'er all its kingdoms reigns.


## 57.

Then through that gloom there beamed a fair young face,
The index of a noble heart; as pure as fair,
And brave as pure ; and she, with seraph grace,
The darkness scattered ; made the desert bear
Sweet flowers that with their fragrance filled the air
Of his sad life.   Bright hope, deep joy, and peace
Her presence brought ; with love's divinest care
She made his sharpest pangs and sorrows cease :
And for the world's contempt, it hurts not hearts like these.

### 58.

She was the angel of his changeful life ;
The blessed messenger of hope and rest ;
Her smile the antidote for fiercest strife ;
Her voice a charm to make the listener blest ;
The radiance of her mild eyes exprest
The heavenly purity and peace within.
" A child of Love and Light," among earth's best,
She from the most degraded hearts could win
Some sparks of the divine, howe'er obscured by sin.

### 59.

And with our lonely, world-forsaken bard
She, with the courage of true love, her fate
For time and for eternity has shared.
What heeded she the bigot's scorn or hate ?
What cared she for the world ? all desolate
The noblest heart 'mong living men she found :
And, like to like, she chose him for her mate ;
And bold and spotless, slander's poison-wound,
She dared for him she loved, and proudly smiled around.

## 60.

But still the sleugh-hounds of the law their prey
With wanton cruelty pursued, and made
His England dark to him.   Away ! away !
For bigotry and malice ne'er delayed ;
And life is precious now.   Come, undismayed,
In other lands, and other climates seek
The peace and rest which cannot be betrayed
To hireling scribes who purchased venom reek
On names and fames 'gainst which all true assaults are weak.


## 61.

So with his one and only treasure, he
Bade to his native soil a last farewell ;
And freedom sought, and found, in lands less free,
Than that which him denied.   Oh, who shall tell
What hope of future joys their bosoms swell,
As o'er the laughing sea their vessel sweeps ;
On what bright visions now their fancies dwell ;—
A home where Love alone a kingdom keeps,
Where peace serenely reigns, and sorrow rarely weeps.

## 62.

On, on they flee ; each all in all to each,

And lacking nothing in each other's eyes ;

Rich in love's smiles, and love's entrancing speech,

The hours, the days pass on in sweet surprise

That earth should still have aught of Paradise,

And they receive a portion of its light.

But o'er them now hangs fairer, bluer skies,

And suns to them beam more than ever bright ;

And their young lives and loves are crowned with new
        delight.

## 63.

Italia, O Italia ! thou hast been,

And art, the land to every pilgrim dear ;

To thee he turns as to his own heart's Queen,

When sorrow needs some lovely thing to cheer.

Thy very name's a charm which exiles hear

With rapture, conjuring up the hour

When greatness was thy playmate ; grace severe

Sat on thy brow ; and earth confessed thy power ;

And beauty then as now was aye thy fatal dower.

## 64.

O land of Art and Song ! Poor chastened one !
The soil where tyrants play their bloody game,
Yet cannot rob thee of thy glories, won
By painter and by poet; for thy fame
Is as a quenchless, still-ascending flame,
And soars beyond the malice, hatred, rage
Of puny despots, whose careers of shame
Shall be the bywords of a coming age,
While thy beloved name will aye men's love engage.


## 65.

And beautiful as beauty's self thou art ;
Adorned with every charm and every grace
That sunny skies, bright hills and lakes impart.
The richest works of Nature find a place
Upon thy fruitful bosom ; rivers trace
Their murmurous courses through the vine-clad plain,
Where winding tendrils fondly interlace
To bear their glowing burdens, whence men strain
The ruby-tinted wine to gladden heart and brain.

## C6.

The land of beauty and of bondage too ;

The land of untold glory and of shame ;

The land whence poets inspiration drew,

And dowered with all their never-dying fame.

The land of deathless memories which inflame

The living with the hope of nobler days,

When Liberty again his home shall claim,

And win once more earth's benison and praise,

Once more be crowned with green as well as faded bays.


## C7.

Unto this land of varied fortunes they

Now turned with hope, and chose it as their own.

Repose and peace are won ; and joys display

Their golden pinions ; flowers are thickly strown

In paths which only wounding thorns had grown ;

And mutual love makes mutual sorrows rare ;

And pleasure smiles as grief had ne'er been known ;

For they are hopeful, joyous, bold to bear ;

Whatever life may bring they can together share.

### 68.

And she was all his dreams had pictured her ;

His dear companion, counsellor and friend ;

Of pleasant fancies the sweet minister :

Her gentle words and gentler actions blend

In loving harmony, and ever tend

His days and hours with high resolves to bless ;

Aye prompting to those noble deeds which lend

A precious meaning unto life ; make less

The things which sadden earth—its pride and littleness.


### 69.

And so they lived with loving for their meed,

The richest earth can give or heaven contain;

And sympathizing with their spirit freed

From fetters man-imposed, which bind, and strain,

And fret the heart to madness, once again

Did Nature smile on them ; all things grew bright,

And river, ocean, mountain, wood, and plain,

In love-created glories richly dight,

Spoke once again to him the language of delight.

### 70.

And children with exhaustless founts of joy,
For ever varying in their power to bless,
With Eden still around them, ere the cloy
Of earthly taint has touched their sacredness,
Were added to their treasures; cheerfulness
Brought to their hearth, where laughter, sport, and song,
And noisy gambols, games of mirthfulness
Which tell the presence of the sinless young,
Gave radiant joy to them who dwelt such scenes among.


### 71.

The pure confiding love of guileless hearts;
The pleasure beaming from bright laughing eyes;
The sweet emotion innocence imparts
To all within its influence; the ties
Of daily budding graces which surprise,
And fill with wond'ring ecstacy; all these,
And all the thousand, thousand charms which rise
Unconsciously where children round the knees
Embracingly will throng, were theirs to cheer and please.

## 72.

And grief, which rends the heart's most hidden chord,
But leaves a pure and chastening peace behind—
The grief by which our tenderest thoughts are stirred,
And all the finest feelings of the mind
Their source, their purpose, and fulfilment find—
The grief which comes when Death with holy hand
Our best-beloved has by his touch divined,
' And, smiling, borne him to the Spirit-land;—
This grief its wisdom brought for them to understand.


## 73.

" The load-star of their lives," their " blue-eyed child,"
While seraph beauty, seraph innocence,
Sat on his sunny brow; ere earth defiled
With its contagious wrongs his heart's defence.
Of childish purity, was summoned hence
To that bright kingdom which awaits the young,
Where all is love, and peace, and joy, and whence,
As in a golden dream of Summer song,
Their voices music blend our darkest thoughts among.

## 74.

They laid their darling in an alien grave,
And planted sweetest flowers above their dead ;
And all that loving hearts could give, they gave
The sacred tears which only parents shed—
With these the unconscious grave they watered;
And hence for them earth had a treasure more.
And though their hearts with bitter anguish bled,
The memory of him was sweet ; the living soar
To where their loveful dead are dwelling evermore.


## 75.

To them he was not dead. And day and night
They heard his sweet voice speaking as of old ;
Beheld his gentle face, and blue eye, bright
With love, and graces full and manifold,
Which had on earth but short time to unfold,
Beam on them gloriously. To hearts that love
There is no death—but change ; and they behold
Their darlings as immortal spirits rove
In realms of beauty, graced with all that bliss can move.

## 76.

And such rich solace came to them in woe,

That sorrow soon in golden robes appears ;

And life, recovered from that piteous blow,

A purer, sweeter, holier aspect wears ;

And eyes dried of their dim suffusing tears

More brightly beam.   All pain is worth its cost ;

All grief is gain ; and in the after years

Its teachings, though severe, are never lost,

But prove a priceless pearl: who has will value most.


## 77.

'Twas so with him.   And year by year his heart

Its suffering told in such exquisite song,

That unto callous souls it could impart

A portion of its beauty; and the throng

Of pitiless abusers owned its strong,

Delicious harmony, its wondrous charm ;

And mourned that unto him could yet belong

A power so thrilling, vengeful hearts to warm

With some sweet touch of love, that made them cease to harm.

## 78.

His themes were glorious as his song was sweet;
Of Truth, and Liberty, and Love his strain;
Of men and women robed and crowned complete
In freedom and in virtue; scorning pain,
And toil, and woe, and torture, to attain
The true heroic height, that earth might be
The blest abode of godlike men, whose reign
Would shatter wrong's all-cursing empiry,
And bring the afflicted joy, and make the captive free.

## 79.

And gathered round him now sweet joy and peace,
Wealth, friendship, hope, content, and glowing fame;
The elevating thought, that ere life cease,
He too might twine the laurel round his name;
A laurel spotless, free from venal shame,
And bright with noble aims, that men might see,
Led by its inextinguishable flame,
That grandeur lies alone in being free,
And love, not power, the all-uniting tie should be.

## 80.

'Twas thus he sung ; such themes inspired his Muse :
Man and man's triumphs in the coming years,
When equal laws, and equal rights infuse
Benignest influences ; and alien fears,
Dread of each other, hate-enforced tears,
Wrong-prompted vengeance, all the evil brood
By passion bred, no more their hydra-horror rears,
To fetter truth, or drown the voice of good,
Or change the flower-sprent earth into a scene of blood.


## 81.

O God! how parti-coloured is the woof
That's woven in the loom of changing Time ;
Now brilliant as the gems of heaven's roof,
Now dark as midnight in a northern clime.
In Summer songs are heard the chilling chime
Of Winter's gloom ; joy's richest laugh contains
A melancholy ring ; good deeds and crime
Tread on each other's heels ; and holy strains
Are preludes oft to lays where sin triumphant reigns.

## 82.

The only thing immutable is death ;
The grave, the sure inheritance of all ;
Nor state, nor rank, nor wealth, nor hope, nor faith,
Can here avail.   This house waits king and thrall.
Stern equalizer, heeding not the call
Of love or hate, of strength or weakness : none
Shall 'scape his hand ; his kindly blow will fall
On every living thing.   The chosen one ;
The gracious power that comes alike to hut and throne.


## 83.

On this alone can man with safety build ;
His every other hope may suffer blight :
Each fondly-cherished trust pass unfulfilled :
Each promised joy prove but a dream of night,
To vanish with the first grey dawn of light :
His aspirations no responses find :
His love repulse : his pleasures no delight :—
But smiling Death will come, the true, the kind,
And with perennial peace bless each afflicted mind.

## 84.

Yet when the gentle messenger shall come,
Blind as we are, we seek his love to shun.
Though all our joys are poor and transient—some
But like a shooting star whose race is run
Ere we can say it is—each foolish one
Will cling with wild tenacity to life ;
Will freely bear its burdens ; with a groan
Repeat its bitter tale of daily strife,
Yet still desire to live with woe and pain so rife.

## 85.

And marvel not.   For who would freely leave
The fields, and streams, and flowers, and light of day,—
All fair and lovely things to which men cleave
With such instinctive joy, and pass away
Into the dark unknown, to be the prey
Of worms, the tenant of the narrow home,
The charnel's inmate, shut from all the play
Of sweet affections, and the joys that come
To earth's most gloomy lot, to life's most fearful doom ?

## 86.

But man, with his immortal yearnings, makes
A spirit-world, more fair and bright than this,
Wherein the soul by flesh untrammelled takes
A nobler flight, and knows a purer bliss ;
Where softer breezes flowers more fragrant kiss ;
Where sin and sorrow come not, and where time,
With all its sad restraints, no longer is ;—
A deathless life, an ever-smiling clime ;
And for a dwelling-place, eternity sublime.

## 87.

With glorious poetry he graces death ;
Of every terror thus he robs the tomb ;
And finds a fragrance in the charnel's breath,
Surpassing all that earth knows of perfume ;
And throws around life's dark and final gloom
Rich halos of such brightness, wealth and power,
The long and unknown valley they illume,
And make more blissful the departing hour,
Than any life could show, when love was in its flower.

## 88.

And thus our poet dreamed ; and with his dreams
Made glorious life, and all that life can show.
He with imagination's piercing beams
Lit up the future, till its wondrous glow
Made beautiful even death, and pain, and woe,
For noble ends sustained ; and o'er the path
Which every foot must tread, his song did throw
A radiance whose heavenly brightness hath
A power to banish fear, or dread of priestly wrath.


## 89.

But oft, in brightest hour of brightest day,
Will suddenly, without forewarning, rise
A fearful tempest that will prostrate lay
The hopes of men ; and, swift as lightning flies,
Will desolation spread, with burning eyes
Consuming harvest's promise—wheat and wine,
And all that yesterday glowed 'neath the skies,
In joy and beauty ; so when bliss divine
Is fullest in the heart, Woe cries, " The hour is mine ! "

### 90.

And unsuspicious of his coming fate,
With heart as buoyant as his hopes were high ;
Blithe as a bird with love and song elate,
He hears with rapture that his friend is nigh,—
Friend of his youth whose friendship dared defy
The scorn, the sneers, the hate of narrow zeal;
And loved when love was rare ; whose open eye
Could worth and genius see behind the veil ;
Whose faith was strong that worth and genius must prevail.

### 91.

And swift o'er Spezzia's bay the vessel flies ;
Her white sails emblems of the hopes she held ;
A picture, 'neath the bright Italian skies,
As beautiful as e'er the eye beheld ;
And joyfully the rich blue waters swelled,
And bore the glad and precious freight along,
While shouts of joy, and peals of laughter welled
From one to joy and laughter strange, whose tongue
Was more familiar far with sorrow's saddest song.

## 92.

But now his hopes are high, his joy intense ;

His spirits mount unto a height of bliss

Which rivals ecstacy.   He knows not whence

Such visitations come ; he knows but this—

That ne'er before such boundless joy was his.

He revels in delight, forgetful so

How fate to him darkly untoward is,

And never yet did bliss on him bestow,

But it foreboding told some great approaching woe.


## 93.

But heedless now of omens, on they sweep,

The dimpling waves against their vessel break

In gentle gurglings as they fain would keep

In unison with laughter.   In their wake

Is left bright silvery lines, which gladly take

The kisses of the sun, and glow with joy :

'Tis gladness, brightness all.   O poet, slake

Your thirst with such delight ; too soon 'twill cloy,

And an o'erwhelming storm these glorious hours destroy.

## 94.

But now in Leghorn's port he safely rides,
And springs with joy upon the welcome shore.
Then, without pause, for Pisa he decides ;
For there are love and friendship, with their store
Of golden hopes, and feelings to tell o'er,
Of all that since their parting has been done ;
Rich thoughts to share ; to heal some eating sore ;
Some wrong to right ; then end as all begun—
Recounting o'er each loss, and o'er each triumph won.

## 95.

Oh, swiftly, far too swiftly flew those days
Of rare enjoyment, and of pleasures rare !
Bright plans were formed of noble themes for lays,
That should for nobler times the world prepare ;
And visions of a future far more fair,
More pure, and more divine, in fancy rose
Among them ; till they saw the world created there
The blest abode of beings who arose
In manhood's godlike grandeur, crushing wrong and woes.

## 96.

Yet this must end. For Mary waits her love ;
And dearer than e'en friendship to his heart,
And reigning far all other power above,
Is her sweet influence ; and he would part
With life and fame to shield from slightest smart
Her gentle, loving soul, that now is stirred
With fancies dim and dire ; thoughts that impart
A sense of coming woe—that breathe no word ;
But shadowy horrors hang about her absent lord.

## 97.

And thus the ever-fatal day is come—
O day of darkness, and O day of woe ! —
Unconscious of the swift impending doom ;
Regardless of the signs the heavens show,
And of the " smoke " which hides the wave below ;
And of the warning of the sailor's tongue.
" The Devil mischief brewing ? " 't may be so ;
But home is sweet, and sweet is Mary's song ;
And omens scare the weak, are conquered by the strong.

### 98.

And seated in his favourite boat once more,
The prow turned homeward, and the heart at rest,
The willing wind swift bears them from the shore,
Where friends are watching with a fear supprest,
And breathing wishes for his safety, lest
That sight should be the last of one so dear.
For, save the most concerned, all feel deprest,
And of some coming danger have a fear,
They vainly strive to quell : here danger is too near :

### 99.

For soon a thick fog covers all the sea ;
And soon that well-watched boat is hid from sight ;
The day is hot ; the breathing is not free ;
No wind is there, the air is still, and night
With preternatural speed wings on his flight ;
The waves seem solid—a lead-coloured mass,
And changed to oily scum their foam of white ;
And now short, panting gusts begin to pass ;
Big rain-drops strike the waves, rebounding as on glass.

## 100.

And swift as frenzy comes the furious storm :

With lightnings flashing, thunder's deadly knell,

Fierce winds, and flooding rains, he rears his form—

The demon of the hour.   'Neath his control

All human strength is weak ; the vessels roll,

Each at his mercy ; his the hand that spares

Or strikes at will ; he takes the part or whole.

None may gainsay him.   Vain are all man's cares :

He comes and blasts his toil, and slays him unawares.*

---

* " On Monday, July the 8th, Shelley and Williams set sail in the *Don Juan* for Lerici.   Trelawny was to have gone with them in Byron's vessel, the *Bolivar*, but was detained for want of some necessary legal permit.   They left about three P.M., when the Genoese mate of the *Bolivar* observed to Mr. Trelawny that they would soon have too much breeze.   Black, ragged clouds were by this time coming up from the south-west ; and the mate, pointing to what he called ' the smoke on the water,' observed that ' the devil was brewing mischief.'   The waves were speedily covered with a sea-fog, in which Shelley's boat was hidden from the view of Mr. Trelawny.   It was intensely hot ; the atmosphere was heavy and moveless to an oppressive degree, and a profound stillness spread far over the ocean.   By half-past six o'clock it was almost dark ; the sea looked solid and lead-coloured ; an oily scum was on the surface ; the wind was beginning to wake, in short, panting gusts ; and big drops of

## 101.

Swift as he came, he leaves that awful scene ;

And all is fair, and calm, and bright again.

The vessels look as if no strife had been,

Spread their white sails, and skip along the plain,

Whose waves in playful gambols make a main

Of sparkling dimples.    Oh, let flow the tear,

And wake the song to sorrow's saddest strain !

Of all the joyous barks once sailing there,

One boat alone is lost—the one we prized so dear !

---

rain struck the waters, rebounding as they fell. 'There was a commotion in the air,' says Mr. Trelawny, who records these particulars, 'made up of many threatening sounds, coming upon us from the sea.' The vessels in the harbour were all in hurried movement, and the tempest soon came crashing and glaring in the fury of thunder, wind, rain, and lightning, over the port and open waters. The storm only lasted about twenty minutes; and during its progress, Captain Roberts watched Shelley's vessel with his glass from the top of Leghorn lighthouse. The yacht had made Via Reggio when the storm began. 'When the cloud passed onward,' writes Mrs. Shelley, ' Roberts looked again, and saw every other vessel sailing on the ocean, except the little schooner, which had vanished.' Mr. Trelawny thought for some time that his friends would return to port; but he waited for them in vain."—*Shelley Memorials, by Lady Shelley*, pp. 196–197.

## 102.

And where is now the precious freight it bore?

O woe of woes, admitting no relief!

And see who roams about that fatal shore

With hair dishevelled, face of marble grief,

And eyes of stony gaze; to doubt, belief,

Alternately the victim and the prey.

In piteous words, as wild as they are brief,

Invoking earth, and heaven, and sea to say

Where is the pearl she seeks, where does her treasure lay.


## 103.

Oh, sorrowing soul that mourns the purest heart

That ever loving woman called her own!

No more his gentle words will joy impart,

No more his glowing tongue in sweetest tone

Will thrill thee with its richness; but alone

Thy life henceforth in changing grief will pass.

No more his face, except in dreams, be shown;

No more, no more shall now be heard, alas!

His voice within the house, his footsteps on the grass.

### 104.

The sea that gorged its prey now casts it forth:
Two mutilated forms lie on the strand;
And one is his—the son of song, whose worth
Men knew too late;—till death's untimely hand
Had borne him to the dark and unknown land,
His greatness was unseen. But there he lies,
In death companioned by the few, who stand
In solemn silence, broken but by sighs,
Which tell how deep their woe, how strong their agonies.

### 105.

These friendly hands erect the fatal pyre;
Bring frankincense, and myrrh, and oil, and wine,
Then to the glorious relics place the fire,
And watch them as they watched a sacred shrine.
For he whose bones consume was half divine;
And as the flames, so did his spirit soar,
And ever toward the godlike did incline;
And, spite of wrongs, himself unsoiled he bore,
And kept aloof from aught that e'er pollution wore.

## 106.

The end is here.  His unconsumed heart
And sacred dust by loving hands were borne
To that sweet spot where lay of him a part,
And by his darling child, his dear first-born ;
And by his favourite bard, a child of scorn
To th' ingrate world, he now in peace is laid ;
And o'er that " heart of hearts," so sadly torn,
The cypress spreads its grand and solemn shade,
And pilgrimages now are to that temple made.


## 107.

Dear child of sorrow, and of song, and light ;
The prophet of a fairer, nobler time ;
The hero of a brave and bloodless fight ;
Dear master of the wonder-waking rhyme,
Who sung the beautiful and the sublime,
Accept this tribute of a later day ;—
The homage of a heart that fain would climb
To higher things, but who, alas! shall say ?—
Upon thy tomb, great bard, this lowly flower I lay.

# THE DEATH OF ST. POLYCARP.

O God, I come to thee, thou art my Life;
O God, thou art my home, I come to thee.

WITHIN AND WITHOUT.

# DEATH OF ST. POLYCARP.

———⋇———

Wide, smooth, and deep is Smyrna's bay,
And stretches far into tho sunny land.
Accepting, as in love, her sweet embrace,
The fair, enamoured earth, with witching smiles,
Her soft arms round the sparkling waters spreads,
And wreathes the rippling waves with richest flowers.

Men coming in from sea are scarce aware
What safe and happy haven waits their sails,
Until within its calm unruffled peace
They quietly repose, and scent the fragrant breeze

Which tells of home, of wife, of child, and friend.
And then before their dim, but gladdened eyes,
Along those pleasant, ever-murmuring waves,
And on those ever-smiling hills—sweet spots
Of beauty and of grace—fair Smyrna stands :
A city to make glad the gazer's heart ;
A city dear unto the memory of man ;
A city sanctified by high heroic deeds,
For ever blazoned by a martyr's blood.

How changed her present from her ancient fame !
Still in the busy streets the merchants throng,
All eager-eyed for gain.   From every land
The venturous and daring gather there,
And haggle with their fellows seeking wealth.
The tongues of many nations still are heard
In loud contention in her public marts,
All trying to outwit, and overreach,
And win the petty triumph of deceit :
A motley, quaint commingling of all garbs,
A picturesqueness lends to what were else
Contemptible and base.   Close, dirty streets,
And houses dull and dismal meet the eye ;
With here and there some remnant of a time

When nobler men were hers, and nobler aims
Inspired her action and her life : when God
Upon the city smiled, and smiling blest :
Another added to that mighty list
Of precious spots whose glory's of the past ;
Whose fame is memory of noble deeds ;
Whose boast is of the what has been,—not is ;
Whose claim upon our reverence and love
Is in the crumbling records which reveal
How once she was a chosen one, and bore brave hearts,
Who dared and suffered for the good of man.

God's gift of beauty is perennial.   The land
He's touched approvingly for ever beams
In all the loveliness of Heaven.   His hand
Of grace and power is seen alike, or in
The dimpling smiles of undulating plains,
By village maidens trod on Summer eves,
Or in the glorious hills that rising, soar
Sublimely in their heaven-seeking heights.
The rippling brook is musical of Him ;
And ever-hymning Ocean sings His praise.
The roadside flower that careless wanderers pass,
Or reckless trample on, reveals His love ;

And Lebanon's far-spreading cedars, swept
By loving winds, are murmurous day and night
Of Him who planted them.   These ever smile,—
Their beauty knows no change: the same to-day
As on Creation's morn, when angels sung
Their joyous, jubilant song ; when heaven was glad
Earth's beauty to behold.

      Not so with man.

He sinks and rises, winning shame and fame—
A glorious, god-like creature, towering, grand,
Majestic; now he takes by right his place
Among th' heroic host ; and now a thing
So mean, so abject, and so vile, the worm
Might scorn companionship with aught so base.
The free-born of to-day, he walks the earth
With step elastic, buoyant as the breeze
Which scarcely bends the flower it stops to kiss ;
Is now a slave so grovelling and so gross,
That vain his God-imparted faculties
To raise him 'bove the beasts with which he wallows,
And takes the curse or stripe as caprice wills,
Or passion prompts, and licks the hand that whips:
So fixed is nature, but so changing man.

And Smyrna still is beautiful, and once
Was grand.   For in her walls she then contained,
And in her streets was daily seen and heard,
The nearest thing to God—a God-like man,
Who rose in all the majesty of love,
Amidst the scorn of all the sinners there,
Protesting 'gainst man's wickedness and sin ;
And preaching unto all the glorious news
Of sweet redemption, and eternal truth,
Of heavenly transports, and immortal bliss :
He spoke of God and His unchanging grace ;
Of Christ and His atoning death ; of love,
Surpassing e'en the mother's for her child ;
Of th' Holy Spirit which awaited all,
And sought but open hearts to enter in.
Of all the glories of the Christian faith
He spoke ; and won, what they have ever won,
Who seek to bless the world and change its
     ways—
The deathless love of some few glowing hearts
With grace to see and strength to love the truth ;
The deathless hate of all the powers that be,
And all they represent, and claim, and guide ;

He won the curse, the shame, the scourge, the death,
The ever-blessed crown of martyrdom.

    Men called him Polycarp.   He had grown grey
In toiling in the vineyard of the Lord.
His years were many, but his heart was young ;
Had firmer hopes of man, and of the world,
Of the high destinies yet waiting them,
Than ever fired the heathen poet youth
Ere he had lost his hot and sanguine years ;
Or the first flow of imaginative blood
Had been by dark experience checked, and turned
To gall, fit but to water wormwood with.
What tinsel was the Golden Age of old
Compared with that which Polycarp revealed!
He, trembling on the verge of years,
With clearer eyes saw sights diviner far,
And visions glorious with God's authentic touch,
Which made him like a child in faith and love,
And heaven a bright reality to win,
Not a fair fable, or divine perhaps,
But an eternal dwelling-place of light,
Made wordlessly magnificent by Him
Who was, and is, and will for ever be

The Source of light, of holiness, and bliss.

The Holy One had met him face to face ;

Had spoke to him, and called him to his work.

He heard and he obeyed.   He chose his task—

Took up his cross, and shrank not from the thorns,

But still with joyous heart, but bleeding brows,

Accepted with a sweet humility

And holy pride the God-appointed lot—

A life of teaching, suffering, and strife ;

A life of peace, and purity, and love ;

A death more glorious than ever crowns

The favoured of the world ; a death reserved

But for the chosen ones who witness bear

To truth before the time is ripe, and men

Have eyes to see.   Such was the lot of Polycarp.

    The world was full of change.   The old and new

In dreadful conflict strove.   All hearts were fired

With frenzied zeal, or high, ascending hopes ;

And raven heads grew hoary in an hour.

The kingdoms of the earth were growing weak,

And in despair a foolish contest waged.

The pagan world was from its centre torn ;

Was sick at heart, and knew not its disease ;

Went raging downward with a show of strength,

Which only told its weakness and its woe ;

Made gibbering faces ; and was loud in cries,

And shrieked in all the impotence of wrath.

For selfishness, and ignorance, and craft,

And evil hopes to keep the growing world

For ever in its chains, had found the way

To win the lovers of the ancient faith :

The earnest and the zealous in the cause

Of gods defunct, and altars without fires.

And these, with all the giddy multitude,

The masses ready still to crown or slay,

As passions skilfully are played upon ;

With rack, and cross, and fire, and boiling oil,

And pincers lacerating to the flesh ;

And savage beasts, by famine fiercer made—

By these, and all the instruments which man,

So quick to answer to the call of hate,

So skilful in providing all the means

To carry out the work which hate suggests,

The pagan world from time to time assailed

The friends of Christ, His teachers, and His faith.

And oft the little seed was steeped in blood ;

And oft the infant Church seemed nigh to death.

But God was faithful to His own.   His hand

Through all the bloody baptisms led them safe ;

And in the darkest hour He lent a light,

Which showed what glorious prospect lay beyond.

For in the midst of pain, and gloom, and death,

His great, grand, loving eye was always there,

And, like a lighthouse to the storm-tossed crew,

Showed where the harbour and where safety lay.

In slavery's sharpest hour, at sorrow's worst,

He gave them courage, strength, and joy ; and still,

Through all His dealings with His chosen ones,

When Pharaoh raged and persecuted most,

He ever sent a Moses to redeem,

And set His people free.

                Once more, once more

The kings of earth were battling 'gainst the Lord ;

Once more His people were oppressed to death ;

Once more He sent His leader forth ; and oh !

Once more the people stoned the prophet ; and

Once more the prophet's triumph was his death.

To such a work the Lord called Polycarp,

And with alacrity and joy he came.

The work performed, received his mead; was blest.
For blest is he who dies in serving God.

    Aurelius ruled in Rome. The noblest head
That ever wore th' Imperial diadem.
Brave, pious, temperate, just, and learned, was he.
The virtues of the pagan world were his.
He loved his people, and revered his gods.
And with a heart of sadness he beheld
The ancient worship and the power of Rome
With equal steps decline. Beheld with awe—
With awe, which no conviction wrought—how grew
In stature and in strength the faith of Him—
The crucified. All this with bleeding heart,
With ever-growing care, and sense of shame,
That men should be so fickle and so vile;
So mindless of their temples and their shrines,
And so blasphemous of the ancient gods,
Whose favouring hands and tutelary care
Had raised eternal Rome, and made her lord
Of all the visible world; oh, he was shamed
That men so honoured had so gone astray!
And with a logic that was partly true and false,
He held the Christians guilty of the change

Which day by day the older faith endured.

To him they were the enemies of the gods ;

The scorners of the old time-honoured rites ;

The mockers of the great Olympian powers ;

The holders of a novel and unholy creed,

Which drew upon the world the withering curse

Of all the high offended deities :

Who for such sins were scourging now the land

With blight, and famine, and disease, and death.

So gathering all his power, he rose, resolved

To vindicate his gods ; to slay their foes ;

And bring once more the reign of piety and peace.

And from his lips the fatal mandate went,

That in all lands acknowledging his rule,

The new faith should be crushed ; the Christians have

But this alternative : to sacrifice

Upon the altar of Almighty Jove,

Or suffer death—death in the sharpest form,

And most enduring agonies, that men,

By hate inspired, and skilful in such work,

Could for the sacrilegious pests invent.

    Then swift as summer-storms, that sweep along

In thunder and in lightning, bearing woe

And desolation on their rapid wings,

And shaking to its centre the sad earth,

O'er which they hang, and burst ; till her sweet face,

So bright with sunny fields, and trees, and flowers,

Is shrivelled into desert barrenness,

And looks in colour as a ten-year corpse :

So swift the mandate of Aurelius flew ;

So dire its work—so fatal its results.

Now, through the streets of Smyrna ran the cry—

" Down with the Atheists !   Away with Polycarp ! "

Th' infuriate mob, by passion roused and fired,

And all unknowing of the things they did,

Went raging up and down, and shrieking still—

" Down with the Atheists !   Away with Polycarp ! "

In every street the welt'ring, seething crowd,

With maddened gestures, and with fiery glare

That shot from cruel eyes, rushed on.   No pause ;

No intercession in their wicked cry :

No sign of pity, and no word of love :

Vindictive all.   The thousands pressing there,

Like hungry beasts in sight of flying prey,

Rush howling on, with deadly hatred filled ;

By unseen terrors goaded, and by vague,

Unutterable fears impelled, they rage

And shriek, all thirsting for an old man's blood.

    And still the cry went forth.  Along the shore

Of Smyrna's far-indented bay, and winding coast ;

Through all the neighbouring woods, and o'er the waste

Which spreads beyond the city, it was heard,

E'en to the distant hills whose echoes rung

The dreadful terror back : and still the cry

Which rung upon the shore, and in the woods,

To silence frightened bird and beast ; which broke

Upon the solitary stillness of the waste,

And gave a thousand voices to the hills,

Each voice a shout for vengeance and for blood,

Was still that fearful and unholy cry—

" Down with the Atheists !  Away with Polycarp ! "

    But Polycarp had fled ; fled not from fear,

For fear of death he knew not ; fear of pain

Had never yet disturbed the old man's ways,

Nor made him falter in his upward course ;

And fear of man was banned by fear of God.

He lived with the Unseen ; and was sustained

By powers invisible to common eyes.

God held him in the hollow of His hand.

He knew that, dead or living, he was safe:
So that the rage of wicked men ; the hate
Of men deluded, sin-enslaved ; the scorn
Which they whose eyes were blinded to the truth,
Had poured upon him ; all the bitter wrongs
Which ignorance and malice did to him ;
The fury still by fury goaded on,
And still intensified by all the strength
Which comes from sympathy in hate,
And spreads contagiously from man to man,
Until the crowd is but one voice, one head, one hand,
Disturbed not his serenity and peace ;
Or moved him but to pity and to prayer.
But fear touched not his God-sustainèd heart ;
Nor shook the steady purpose of his life.
Yet Polycarp had fled.   For he had heard
His Master's voice ; and knew his Master's words ;
And knew that He had work for him to do,
Which it were sinful pride to shun.   And so
When rose that vengeful cry from those he loved,
For whom he toiled and prayed, and who to him
Were more than life or death, the old man fled—
Fled, though he thirsted for the martyr's crown,

And for that blessed gift had day and night
With far more passionate fervour prayed,
Than ever lover yet to clasp his bride.
But still he waited the appointed time ;
Still bore his cross ; and left it to God's will,
Life's burden when to take away, and when
To robe him in the spotless robes of death.
    His flight stayed not the fury of the mob.
A moment baffled, they were not appeased.
The pause was like a little water thrown on fire ;
The flames which are not quenched more freely spread,
And so the people's passions rose to learn
Their victim had escaped.   The news flew fast ;
The cry rang louder ; fiercer the pursuit.
Blood was their want ; for all too long their eyes
On cruel scenes had gazed : and all too oft
Their ears been charmed with piercing shrieks, and
        groans
Of agony from suffering weakness forced,
To let their prey escape.   He was pursued.
And wild as hounds that once the scent have had,
And lost, with varied cries the furious men,
In furious packs, went bellowing to and fro ;

With many windings in and out ; with doublings
And returnings back and back again, they searched
All likely and unlikely spots, and made
A pastime of their cruel hunt ; and each
His neighbour's zeal, which needed not such help,
Was fanning with his loud halloo, and voice
Of wild encouragement, and bitter words,
Provocative of still-increasing rage.
Thus on they went, nor slackened in their quest,
Until they lighted on the hiding-place
The holy man had found.

                  His time was come.
He knew his time was come, and he rejoiced.
The hour for which his heart so oft had yearned ;
His hour of triumph and of death was come,
And soon the Crown were his.   So he rejoiced.
He waited not that men should drag him forth,
But walking in his Master's foretrod path,
His life would of his own free will lay down.
With quiet mien, with loving, gentle look,
Did Polycarp to meet his foes come forth.
At sight of him, so calm and so benign,
The furious crowd were into silence hushed.

None knew the cause ; but as he gazed on them—

His grey beard lovingly kissed by the wind,

Which seemed to linger there in sweet delight ;

His furrowed forehead, high and reft of hair,

Before them bared ; his kind and hopeful eye

With overflowing kindness on them bent—

It was as if a hand unseen were laid

Upon their mouths, and all their voices hushed.

The glaring eyes were settled in their gaze ;

And all the passion-flurried faces fixed

In wond'ring admiration.   On them fell

An influence as sweet, as rage-subduing,

As that, which in a summer twilight steals

Into the mind, lays its balmy hand on care,

And gives the heart a transient feeling of

The pure serenity of Heaven.   They stood,

Despite themselves, subdued to quietness.

And when his cheerful voice proclaimed himself,

And craved the boon, a little time for prayer,

A little time to supplicate his God,

And gather strength to fit him for his end,

No voice was lifted up against his wish ;

And so the Christian won.

                                    Long time he prayed.
For two rich hours his spirit left the earth,
And held communion with God.   His voice,
So often exercised in prayer and praise,
Serener rose in this his peril time,
Than when in safety and in peace.   His foes,
Made callous by repeated wrongs, grew mild,
And listened wond'ringly, that one so old,
Surrounded by the messengers of death,
And threatened with a fierce and cruel end,
Could thus forget himself.   He prayed for all:
The weak, the groaning, persecuted Church—
The poor, afflicted brethren in the Faith—
His foes, who raged, not knowing what they did.
He prayed for all; and, lastly, for himself:
For strength to bear whatever pain and shame,
The rage of frenzied fancy could suggest,
The cruelty of savage hearts inflict;
For thus sustained all suffering would be bliss,
And he should die rejoicingly; should pass
With prayer upon his tongue, smiles on his lips;
Nor bring disgrace upon the infant faith,
Nor prove unworthy of his Lord and Christ.

Then calmly came the old man forth.  His face
Shone gloriously bright ; and from his eyes
A heavenly splendour beamed.  E'en so of old
The favoured Moses looked, when from the fire
Upon Mount Sinai's height he turned
And gazed upon the people.  So looked he :
But all the terror softened and subdued
Into a sweet, celestial grace, which told
That Sinai's thunders, Sinai's law, no more
Came threatening unto man : but in their stead
The blessed Gospel sealed upon the cross ;
The burden light of mercy, faith, and grace.
So calmly came the old man forth—no shout,
No cry of loud, exulting foes—no sign
Of gratified revenge—now greeted him.
In silence the proconsul's soldiers came
And met him ; placed him on an ass ; and thus,
As rode the Holy One, but without pomp
Of gladdened maidens strewing flowers along,
Or loud hosannahs singing as they went,
Tho fond disciple journeyed to his doom.
    They journeyed slowly on.  Serene and glad
The willing martyr rode.  Before him rose,

As in a happy vision, all the past;

And unto him, as to a dying man,

The years came back.   As in an open book,

With pictures filled, illuminations fair,

And records of the days bygone, he read;

And thus re-lived it all.   The blessed hours

Of childhood nestled in his sunny home,

Cheered by a mother's love, a father's care.

And all the sweet solicitude which clings

About a favourite child, returned to him.

And once again he sported with his toys,

And prattled pretty nothings all the day.

And now he listened to those heavenly words,

The prayer his mother taught his infant lips;

And on his knees, his little upraised hands

Still resting on her lap ; his wond'ring eyes

Fixed largely on her love-revealing face.

His lisping tongue is striving to repeat

Her words ; his little mind to understand

Their blessed meaning, and to catch their charm.

Which made his mother's face so full of joy ;

So beautiful to look upon ; so rich

In graces indescribable ; lit up

With a celestial brightness, which he saw
And loved, but scarcely knew the source. And then
Remembrances of all that precious time,
Came crowding, likest angels, on his mind,
And all that since had been. But chiefest rose
Those priceless interviews which erst he had
With that disciple whom the Saviour loved,
Who laid his head upon the Saviour's breast,
And afterwards those wondrous things beheld
Which God revealed to him alone at Patmos.
The present in the past he lost. His mind
With high and holy thoughts was lifted up,
The doom prepared for him he heeded not,
The death of shame was glorified to him.
For all the ignominy heaped on him
Would make the mercy sweeter in the end;
And for the crown of martyrdom on earth,
The crown of glory waited him in heaven.
The hungry beasts might rend his weak old limbs;
The hungrier flames might scorch his wrinkled flesh;
The boiling oil might shrivel up his frame;
The cruel pincers rend him bit by bit;
But this would end. The bitter pain would pass;

The agony so fearful for the flesh,
God helping, could be borne.   The anguish o'er,
The bitterness of suffering once endured,
The end were reached ; the long-sought goal attained ;
The victory won ; eternal peace secured,
And bliss that never ends ; the song of praise
Which white-robed angels and redeemèd saints
Sing round God's throne for ever, then begin,
And he a singer there !

                 With such high thoughts,
With boundless hopes, and joy unutterable,
Saint Polycarp rode on.   His gentleness
Subdued his captors' passions.   Low they spoke ;
Forgot their wonted callousness of words,
And laid aside the rudeness of their trade.
They saw the calmness in their prisoner's face,
And whispered admiration.   Astonished heard
With what serenity he spoke ; how free from fear,
How with untrembling limbs he rode to death :
They saw the unwonted brightness of his eyes,
The glory hanging round him and his beast ;
And so in wond'ring silence all rode on.

   In the arena Rome's proconsul sat ;

His guards and lictors, symbols of Rome's power,

Surrounded him. And there assembled, too,

All Smyrna's priest-encouraged multitudes,

Impatient of delay. But loudest rose the cries

For blood from the descendants of the race

That crucified the Lord, and Stephen stoned.

Of all that frenzied crowd the Jews were heard

Most fiercely shrieking for the martyr's death.

And when the melancholy cavalcade

First met the sight of that assembled host,

As from one mouth in unison arose

One deep, intense, and murder-freighted shout,

Announcing that the sport would soon begin.

But Polycarp, unmoved and undisturbed,

And praying for his foes, rode to his doom.

The smile of deep beatitude still played

About his lips ; and all his bearing showed

The peaceful soul within. Absorbed in prayer,

He moved along : to him nor cries, nor rage,

Nor fear of torture came. His hope was sure,

Fixed on th' Eternal's word, that could not fail.

And now, when most such help was needed him ;

When through the flesh's weakness shame might come.

Divine assurance, such as God imparts
To His selected saints, was favoured him.
For from the cloudless heavens came a voice—
" Be strong, and be a man, O Polycarp ! "
The many heard the sounds : but words alone,
In their distinct articulation, reached
The chosen one.   He heard and was renewed—
Before his eyes, invisible to those
By passion blinded, hung God's mighty shield ;
A guardian angel hovered over him.
The heavens were opened to his ravished sight,
And he beheld the bright, white throne of God,
And all the elders round it.   On the right
Sat He, his Lord, his Saviour, and his Christ.

Before the judgment-seat the martyr stood :
The courteous Roman, moved by his grey hairs,
Forgot the sternness of the judge.   In words
Of gentleness, and mild entreaty, he,
With th' old man, pleaded for the old man's life.
" Have pity on thy age," he said, " and swear
By Cæsar's fortune.   Leave thy foolishness ;
Forget thy God—or what thou tak'st for such—
And cry with me—' Away with the Atheists ! ' "

Then Polycarp to his full height arose,

His radiant face upon the people turned,

And looking up to heaven, cried aloud—

" Away with the Atheists ! "

                        Then said the judge—

And smiled at victory so easily won—

" Now take the oath ; deny this Christ, and free

Art thou for ever."

                  But with unfaltering voice,

And words of calm severity, the saint :

" For six and eighty years Him have I served ;

For six and eighty years has He been pleased

To bless that service, doing me no wrong.

Shall I speak evil of my Lord and King ? "

    But still with gentleness, and kindly voice,

As all reluctant to condemn, the judge :

" Then swear by Cæsar's fortune."

                      He replied :

" If but for idleness thou urgest this ;

Or out of kindness, from a noble heart,

And having pity on my years, still seek'st

To satisfy thy nature and the law,

Nor yield unto this savage cry for blood,

Accept my thanks.   But if, not knowing me,
Nor what the faith I hold, in ignorance
Thou speak'st; persuading me for ease,
Or profit, or the base desire of life,
To do unholy and accursed things,
Pernicious to the soul, and worse than death ;
'Tis time to undeceive thee.   Hear me then :
I am a Christian.   More, if thou would'st learn
Of me, and of my faith, grant me but time ;
And all its blessings, all its boundless wealth—
Of mercy and of love, its inward peace
Which passeth understanding, and its bliss,
Which, when this weary life is laid aside,
This wicked world, its pomps, and vanities,
And its illusions, all are past away,
Endures for ever and for ever—hear,
And I will teach."

                    But he, evading, said :
" Persuade the people."

                    Then with calm dignity,
And voice of one who knew how vain the task,
To any but the Lord Omnipotent
To bid the tempest-raging sea be still,

With reverence said : " My mouth is closed for them.

But unto thee, clothed with authority,

And bearing on thy brow the seal of Rome,

And her imperial greatness, and to whom,

As one ordained and ratified of God,

Respect, allegiance, honour, all are due,

I would explain the faith ; and win, perchance,

A noble soul from death.   But unto these,

With hate and long-delayed revenge enraged,

I nothing owe.   Them I may not persuade."

Perplexed, and waxing wroth, the Roman then:

" Wild beasts, the savagest, and newly caught,

Their native desert fury in them still,

And fiercer made by two days' hunger-pangs,

Await my nod to rend thee limb from limb.

Reflect, old man.   Be placable to me ;

But more, be placable unto thyself,

And do this harmless thing."

                      " It is not good,"

With sudden animation, said the saint,

"Thy Roman poets say it is not good,

To leave the better for the worse, and I

The better path have chosen all too long,

Have too few years between me and the grave,
To learn to walk in any other.   No more :
I will not change."
                    In sterner mood the judge :
" Thy blood on thy own head.   But witness bear,
How, moved to pity by thy noble mien,
That venerable aspect, those grey hairs,
So like the few which crown my father's years,
I've sought thy peril to avert.   But now
The slow-consuming fire must be the charm
To burn this stubborn spirit out.   And thou,
Not I, the guilt—if guilt there be—must bear,
Of its necessity.   I can no more."
                         Then he,
With smile of sweet compassion, and with voice
Of sunny tenderness : " My thanks are thine
For this thy mercy, and mistaken care.
But know the fire thy order kindles here
Is quenched before the night ; the pain thy hands,
Or their most subtle instruments, can give,
Ends in a little time, and is no more,
But, oh, there is a fire that burns for ever.
Not all the waters of the many seas

Can quench that sin-fed flame.   There is a pain
Which never ends ; a worm that never dies.
Poor were my gain to win eternal loss,
By 'scaping such a doom as thou and those
Can, at its worst, inflict.   But this, alas!
Thou know'st not of, and wilt not know.   Blind, deaf,
With all thy senses closed to truth, thy lot,
Thus great with greatness, and the pomp of power,
Is wretchedness itself compared with mine.
Alas, I pity thee ; and weep for thee ;
And mourn thy loss.   But now, why parley I ?
Why tarriest thou ?   Do with me as thou wilt ;
I am a Christian."

      The sign and word were given ;
The herald's voice proclaimed unto the crowd
The martyr's guilt ; his punishment proclaimed.
" He is a Christian ; he has confessed ; and now
The stake and fire are his."   Then rose the cry,
" Away with Polycarp !   The stake ! the stake !
Let him be burnt alive ! "

       Unmoved, the saint
Heard all their cries ; and saw their eager zeal,
Unmoved.   As ocean's billows rolling, rise

With the increasing storm, and rise and roll
With white-lipped fury foaming; so the crowd,
Each one desiring to behold the game,
And see the crowning glory of the sport,
Rose surging up, and rolled in billowy waves,
With thunderous execrations, white and wild;
And as the rock, against whose hoary sides
They, threatening desolation, madly dash,
Smiles calmly grand to see them at his feet
Break into harmless spray: so looked, so smiled
The dying man upon that multitude
Of up-turned faces, cursing, mocking him,
And pressing to behold his awful doom.
But he was strong in God.

     And save his God,
No help was there to cheer him or console.
A few of his own faith, but lacking strength
To bear the martyr's death and win the crown,
Which swift as flies the arrow to his mark
Had been the meed of recognition there,
Held back, and mourned in secret for their priest,
And offered up their silent prayers for him,
And asked for him the courage they had not.

But yesterday, the weakest there had said
What joy it were to bear and die as he.
But terror held them now, and checked the voice,
And froze their courage in its fount.   Alone,
Alone for mortal counsel, mortal help,
The old man stood ; alone and near his death.
    The stake was raised.   And with the speed of hate,
The unanimity of men in wrong,
All rushed to aid the work.   Some faggots brought,
And piled them round the stake ; some broken casks,
And forms, and chairs, and implements of wood ;
Some poured on tar ; some quenchless turpentine :
Some made them torches of the free-brought hemp ;
Some brought the ropes to bind him to the stake ;
Men, women, little children even joined the work,
And each 'gainst each with bitter envy strove,
Who most his hatred and his zeal should show.
So all that ruthless crowd, swayed by one thought,
Inspired by one absorbing aim, and led
By fierce unbridled passion, thus became
An old man's executioner.
                        The work went on.
But he, the victim of this fatal haste,

Stood rapt in all the ecstacy of prayer.

He heeded not these fearful preparations.

His eyes were fixed on heaven, and his heart

Received the strength of those who trust in God.

He held his hands in supplicating form,

But not to man.   He asked no mercy there.

And when he looked to earth, undaunted he

Beheld the stake, the gathering heaps of wood,

The furious diligence of all the crowd

In hastening on the moment of his death,

And smiled to think how glorious to him

Would prove what they for punishment and shame

Devised.   All is prepared ; and now approach

The executioners to bind him to the stake.

And then the spirit of the saint arose,

Repelled this last indignity, and said—

"No fetters.   Leave me thus.   The God above

Who gives me strength to bear the fatal fire

Will give me strength unfettered and unbound

To stand and burn.   Let me in freedom die."

   With joy, and something of alacrity,

He walked to death.   And as they lit the pile

Again he lifted up his voice in prayer,

And thus his supplications rose to heaven :

" Lord God Omnipotent !   My gracious God,

The Father of our blessed Saviour Christ,

Through whom our knowledge of Thy mercy comes ;

O ! Lord of Lords, and King of Kings ; the One

And only God, Creator of the world

And Lord of all the visible universe,

Of all the generations of the dead,

Of all the righteous who before Thee bow ;

Lord God of Might, of Mercy, and of Love,

I thank Thee for the honour of this day ;

That Thou hast thought me worthy of this death ;

Worthy to be a witness of the Faith ;

Worthy to drink my portion of that cup

Once drained by Him who died upon the cross—

Who died for me, for these, for all mankind,

And gave Himself a sacrifice for sin,

That we might praise Thee with eternal life.

Oh, take me, Lord, unto Thyself.   Accept

This poor return for all Thy love, and take

My sinful, sorrowing soul into Thy care.

Let it be found acceptable to Thee.

O God, the only faithful, only true,

Reject not these my supplications, made
In hope, in firm reliance on Thy word,
Which never yet deceived; but is the same
From everlasting unto everlasting.
With this my latest breath I praise and bless,
And thank Thee; glorify Thy name; and trust
That ere this ever-blissful day shall end
My soul shall with the saints and elders join
In praising Thee for evermore.    And Lord
For these misguided men, whose cruel hands
Administer my death, whose cruel hearts
Are hungering for my end; forgive them all.
They know not what they do.    Impute it not
Against them on Thy Judgment Day.    Their hate
Is prompted by the Evil One, Thy foe.
Let him not triumph with their erring souls.
Forgive them, Lord, and me.    Let it be so."

His prayerful voice had scarcely ceased to plead,
When the impatient crowd with torches rushed
To fire the patient pile.    Then swiftly spread
The forky tongues as greedy to devour him.
With every crackling of the hungry fire,
And every soaring of the eager flame,

Fierce shouts, and cries, and loud hurrahs arose.

But with upraisèd hands the martyr stood,

Serene and joyous, smiling through the flames,

Which, as a garment, clothed him round about,

And still more fiercely raged and raged, and rose

More loftily above the stake.　But, lo!

As they his body would consume, some power

Repelled them back; and round that holy form,

And o'er his head, they spread like golden wings

Protecting, glorifying thus the chosen one.

The wondrous spectacle made silent e'en

That reckless crowd: for all with awe beheld

The miracle—the victim unconsumed.

The burning element reft of its power,

Innocuous was, and harmless to the man

On whom the Lord had placed His panoply

Of grace.　And thus his spirit passed to Heaven.

No pain was his. No torture he endured.

Man's rage was conquered by the love of God.

The Saviour he confided in was there

His dear disciple to protect and bless:

And thus his faith was crowned. Oh, not in vain

Had he resigned himself: and not in vain

His hand placed in his heavenly Father's hand,
Confiding in His guidance through the world!

One wonder more!   The saint was doubly owned
A chosen child of God.   And, oh, once more,
That wicked generation saw the love
The Father for His children bears; again
A sign was given; and again men saw
The veil removed from the invisible,
And heavenly glories manifest to all.
For ere the spirit of the martyr left
His tabernacle of the flesh, the clouds
Were held apart; and for a little time
The splendours of the house of God revealed;
And from the inmost altar, lo, a dove,
A snow-white dove, descended, clad in light:
And round and round the flame-enshrined head
In radiant circles flew.   And as the saint
Thus promise-rich, with joy gave up the ghost,
Went swiftly back to God.

                   And thus in faith,
In patience, in humility, and hope,
By miracle approved, died Polycarp.

# MISCELLANEOUS POEMS.

7

Oh, green is the colour of faith and truth,
And rose the colour of love and youth,
    And brown of the fruitful clay.
Sweet Earth is faithful, and fruitful, and young,
And her bridal day shall come ere long,
And you shall know what the rocks and streams
    And the whispering woodlands say.

REV. C. KINGSLEY.

# MISCELLANEOUS POEMS.

## Wedded and Buried.

THE sun came gladly back that sweet Spring morn :
And, as he rose above the hill which stands
The glorious guardian of our village homes,
And flooded all the valley with his light,
There from our venerable steeple came
The merry peal of bridal-bells, which sent
A thrill of joy through every cottage hearth,
And made the little children shout with joy—
A shout as pleasant as the marriage bells—
Their mothers watching with such happy looks,
You knew they thought of that all-hopeful day,

7—2

So many, many years ago, when the dear name
Of Love into the dearer one of Wife
Was changed.   The village seemed lit up with joy ;
The hills became reverberant with joy ;
The lovely valley smiled more beautiful
Than e'en her wont ; and yet she always was
The fairest valley that fair England boasts.
But now a grace was added to her charms :
She seemed endowed with sense to know and feel
And sympathize with human bliss ; and had
In this our merry-making a large share,
And clad herself in garments royal rich ;
Adorned her smiling brow with precious gems ;
And held her bright face up unto the sky
So full of gentle loveliness, that I,
Who had from boyhood loved and dwelt with her,
With every phase of her excelling beauty
Had, day and night, held converse, now beheld
Th' unusual glory there with joy as fresh
As when at first my eyes were blest enough
To see how beautiful she was.   She lay,
Her bright face smiling on the brighter sky,
And unto my enraptured eyes she grew

More bright, more beautiful, as through the air—
Which murmured sweetly as it kissed her face—
There came the merry sound of bridal-bells.

    The birds sang merrily as rose the sun,
And careless to a careless world revealed
The depth of bliss with which love fills the heart;
From every tree they carolled forth their joy;
Unto the topmost note of exultation
Each warbler told his love. The gentle winds,
As sound-enamoured, gladly bore away
The thrilling strains, and all the air with song
Was musical. It was the time of love,
And earth was in her bridal-robes. The flowers,
Released from Winter's cold embrace, came forth
To greet with grace and beauty joyous Spring,
Who looked on them and smiled. Oh, such a smile!
So full of genial warmth, so sunny bright,
So motherly and cheering none could help,
But blossom forth in gladness when she came.
The clustering primrose jewelled every bank,
Aye wooing venturous children up its side
To pluck the envied treasure. The violets
Their fragrance breathed unseen, and let their sweets

Come giving joy to all; themselves content
To be the unobtrusive ministers
Of pleasure unto others—like good deeds done
By pious Christian souls.   The hedgerows smiled
Their brightest green, and budded into leaves
Exquisitely adorned.   The orchard-trees,
Clad then in all the hues of promise, gave
Their beauties to the passing winds, which bore
The sweet and delicate apple-blossoms far
And near, and filled the air and strewed the ground
With petals soft and rich as fairy-wings.
And round the cottage walls the plum-trees hung
Their thick and clustering bloom.   The earth was gay
In rich and varied tints; and brightly looked,
With half-coquettish, half-enamoured eyes,
Upon the bright face of th' o'erarching heavens,
Which smiled on her again.

                  And over all,
And adding to the glory of the scene,
Still from our venerable steeple came
The merry peal of bridal-bells.

                      The sun,
The song of birds, the spring flowers, and the bells,

The mild and genial breezes, fragrance-laden,

Had wooed me from my solitary room.

I, careless, half-unconscious, without aim,

Then rambled on through our kine-pasturing fields,

Adown our sweet and pleasant lanes, by trees

O'erarching, quietly secluded, made

The very spots where lovers love to walk,

To share alone the glad confessions which,

As far too blest for words, are whispered low,

Though none be there to hear.   Along the side

Of our belovèd streamlet, rippling on

Its music-making way 'tween banks, by flowers,

And water-kissing shrubs, and drooping trees

Rejoicing in their mirrored beauty, lined.

Then on the narrow footbridge resting, I—

As oft through all the changes of the year—

Stood idly watching the bright waters flow;

The rapid minnows sparkling in the sun ;

Or, in vain terror, rushing past in shoals

Which make the waters dark.   The sweet white flowers

Which peer above the rippling waves and smile

From out their dark green shields, like fairy heads

Seen in poetic dreams among the grass.

The yellow king-cups brighter than the gold
Upon an Emperor's crown. The reeds, which bring
To mind the blest Arcadian days of Pan,
When he upon them played, and charmed the world;
And which, now by the playful breezes stirred,
Give forth a music full as sweet and rich
As any which the Greek god from them drew.
The water-flies with bright and gauzy wings
That restless dart from side to side, and glow
Like wingèd emeralds in the early sun.
The bits of grass, the petals freshly shed,
The fallen leaf, and other strays and waifs,
Which on the streamlet's buoyant bosom borne,
Sail lightly by. In reverie I stood,
And watched the calm unconscious life,
Whose fair existence, without pain or fear,
But full of beauty, and a changeful joy,
Lay breathing there before me. I stood and watched,
And from our venerable church again,
But in a louder and more jubilant swell,
There came the merry peal of bridal-bells.

I left the bridge, and crossed the narrow field
Which lies between it and our ancient church.

A hundred villages in England are adorned

By such a holy house.   Upon a hill

It stands; with trees surrounded ; from afar

You only see a graceful spire uprise

Behind their green ;—a blessed sight, and one

Which with the eloquence of silence points

For ever and for ever up to God.

A dark and densely-branchèd yew its gloom

Upon the old and crumbling tombstones throws.

Its walls are full of time-flaws, tinted o'er

With that exquisite colour painters love.

Its weather-eaten dial on sunny days

Still marks the course of time, and kindly points,

With noiseless hand, to that eternity

Which every moment nears.   Around the porch—

The quaintly ancient porch—and up the walls

The ruin-loving ivy thickly grows,

And clothes them in a robe of deathless green :

While from the porch unto the outer gate

Two rows of linden lovingly embrace

And make a covered path, so beautiful

That worshippers oft linger at the door,

And from its blessed calm receive a grace,

And preparation fit for coming prayer.

Around it now our villagers were met,

Clad in their best, and all with smiling looks

And merry voices spoke.   The children held

Sweet nosegays in their hands; and on the floor

Fresh-gathered flowers and sparkling evergreens

Had thickly strewn.   For Clara was our pride—

The village favourite, beloved of all;

And soon as rose the sun they were abroad,

To show by little kindly acts, how dear

She was; how much her happiness was hoped;

And how delighted were her friends that morn

To hear the merry sound of bridal-bells.

    The bridal party came.   And never yet

Has eye of man beheld a fairer form

Than that young bride's.   Her dark and shining hair

In long and flowing tresses almost hid

The perfect outline of her glorious neck.

Her fair cheek, tinted with a maiden blush,

Was more than fair.   The brightness of her eyes

Their long and tremulous lashes hid, as low

She bent them timorous on the ground.   She walked

So like a thing of light, of love, and joy,

That one the idle fancy might forgive
Which deemed her not of earth.   As thus she passed
All voices asked a blessing on her head,
And for her happiness to Heaven prayed.
She raised her eyes a moment on them all
And thanked them so.   It was enough ; for thanks
So full of gentle trust words could not speak ;
And crowned with blessings, Clara, hopeful, went
Into the holy place.
                              Until that day
I had not seen the bridegroom.   He had come,
A stranger to us all—was rarely seen—
Yet had our richest treasure won—was now
The sole possessor of the purest gift
God gives us in this world.   I liked him not ;
There was a hardness in his face ; his eye
Was wandering, seeking to avoid your look ;
And round his mouth a soft and silky smile,
In which his heart shared not, for ever played.
Deep lines—but not the lines which sorrow makes,
Nor those more venerable, the work of age—
His cold and selfish-looking visage marred.
He looked upon our presence with a lour,

And seemed to envy her, his chosen one,

His soon to be all-loving, trusting wife,

The favours and the friendship of her peers.

I turned and left the place.   My heart was sad;

My fears rose spectre-like before my eyes :

A married widowhood of painful years

I augured for our darling and our pride.

I grieved for her.   And never more that day

For me came music with the marriage bells.

    \*      \*      \*      \*      \*

The Spring had passed.   And Summer—who, most like

A queenly mother on our valley smiled,

And crowned with royal gifts the favoured spot—

Had heard the steps of Autumn on the air,

And o'er her shoulder turned her glowing face,

Reluctantly departed.   The birds were gone—

All, save the winter-loving robin, and

A few lone sparrows chirping from the caves,

Had sought a land not reft of Summer's sun.

The early-shedding elm had cast its leaf,

And every glorious tint which Nature's hand,

With her infinity of skill, delights to paint,

Our little coppice showed.   The chesnuts hung

Right in the face o' the sun their bursting nuts,

Whose glossy brown as brightly sparkled there

As dark-eyed maidens of the sunny South,

When meeting those they love.  Where'er you trod

The prickly-sheathèd treasures thickly lay;

And as you meditative walked along

A breeze would shake them, bursting from the
    tree;

Or strew your path with crisp and airy leaves

Which rustled a sweet music 'neath the foot.

The firs their penetrating branches spread,

Cone-laden, dark, erect, and wind-defiant,

Upon the Autumn scene, and gave the charm

Of rich variety so dear to man.

Above, the fleecy and fantastic clouds,

Assuming shapes of all created things,

Or those imagination bodies forth—

The lovely, the grotesque, the wild, the fair,

The fairy light, and gorgeously sublime,

All tinted by an ever-varying sun

Sailed swiftly by.  It was a picture far

Surpassing all that visioned fancy paints,

For it was real.  I saw it there that morn

Created, glorified, just as it came
Directly from the mighty hand of God.

That Autumn morn so golden and so bright
Found all our valley shadowed o'er with gloom,
And every inmate sad. The very young
Had from their elders caught the trick of grief,
And spoke in solemn whispers, looking grave.
The mothers pressed their infants to the breast
To still their cries while they had time to weep.
E'en hardy men, not moved by common griefs,
And unaccustomed sorrow's power to feel,
Looked softened and subdued almost to tears.
Our village bells, unconscious instruments
Of grief or joy, and which, with brazen tongue,
A few, few months ago, had filled the air
With merry peals, which found responsive joy
In every heart, now slowly, solemnly,
With dirge-like sound, the very note of woe,
The awful death-knell tolled. The selfsame bells
Which then our Clara's marriage morning hailed,
Now rang the requiem of her early death.

I could not join the sad and mourning throng,
But turned my back upon the blessed spot

So soon the precious treasure to possess
Of her, whom as a brother I had loved—
Loved as a brother whom no sister knew ;
And had from childhood called the dead one so.
I left the village, thinking of the past
And all its broken hopes.   Still on my ear
The dreary tolling fell, each sound a heart-ache.
I neared our wood, and sought my favourite spot—
Oh, such a spot !   Man's eye but rarely sees,
Man's heart is rarely cheered by such a scene.
Here Oberon might have held his fairy court ;
And here Titania tripped with him in dance
To elfin music heard by few.   To me
It long had been familiar ; solitude
Spent here was full of pleasant thoughts and joys.
Three noble chesnuts' interlacing arms
A semicircle made of shaded grass.
Along the base there slept a silent pool,
Whose waters held a copy of the towering trees,
So clear that every flutter of a leaf
Wind-kissed was tremulous seen within.
For hours and hours and hours I've stood and watched
That scene until it all miraculous seemed,

And not of earth.   Now, on this Autumn morn,

Its beauty and its glory were increased.

It was as if *her* spirit smiled on all,

And breathed through every object there.   The leaves

Were of all hues—from heaven's serenest gray

To deepest green, and richest sun-set gold;

And as the winds among them gently played,

And shook them lovingly, they, tremulous,

In showers of softly-intermingling tints,

Like gems in Eastern tales, about me fell.

All things were with the feelings of the hour

In deep and seeming-conscious harmony.

The trees, the leaves—the falling and the fallen—

The cast-off nuts which crunched beneath my tread,

The calm and silent pool, the quiet sky,—

Seemed parts of that sad ceremony which

That moment witnessed in our church, from whence

The wind the deep and solemn music brought,

Which now came to me like a voice of joy.

'Twas as I feared.   Poor Clara, in the wealth

Of conscious innocence and maiden love,

Had clothed her bridegroom with the robes

Which her own fancy wove; had given him

The virtues which her gentle nature loved,
But his did not possess. In boundless hope
She wedded an ideal which all too soon
Betrayed its common earth. The spell was snapt;
The idol broken; and she knew the pang—
The life-destroying pang of those who love,
Yet scorn the thing they love.

     Oh, those few months!
What agony, what shame, what pains intense,
Were crowded in that little, little space.
A life of woe drawn to the utmost term
Allowed to our mortality could scarce
Have held such woe.

    I wept to think of it.
He was not of the mould to mourn, and kept
Through all a calm, unruffled look which mocked
The wrong he'd done. His lips ne'er lost the smile
Which on his bridal morn around them played.
He ne'er was moved to passion; never said
Or did a thing which seemed to strangers harsh.
But he was selfish—selfish through and through.
Each thought was self; each word and deed were self.
She was a toy, a servant, or a slave,

As each capacity best ministered

To his still changing whim.   And calm and cold,

His manner, far more cruel than his words,

Chilled her young love e'en in its very founts.

She murmured not ; nor breathed aught of complaint ;

But passed away, as passes some sweet flower

Of sunnier lands brought to our northern clime.

One poor request she made—that she might sleep

Where slept the father who had cared for her,

The mother whom she loved.   And this was done.

Thus died our village favourite and pride.

Before the world had sullied her sweet life,

The hand of time, relentless in its touch,

Had marred the beauty of her early years.

They summoned her where beauty never fades,

Where selfishness and sorrow never come.

A married widowhood of painful years

My unforeseeing fears had prophesied ;

But God was merciful, and in His love

Had called her home.

                 And thus that tolling bell

A far more joyous music brought to me

Than did the ringing of her marriage peal.

# The Village Fountain.

———◦◦◦———

Our fountain lords it in the market-place,
    And from a lion's mouth its waters flow
On writhing fish, wrought with such wondrous art,
    You almost doubt are they alive or no.
And round its conch-like basin, day by day,
    The village gossips gather, young and old;
And all our village life is canvassed there,
    And all its doings and misdoings told.


There grave and gay, and blithe and sad, are met;
    The comedy and tragedy of life;
The little cares and sorrows that oppress;
    The hopes that lend a glory to its strife.

S—2

Of births, and deaths, and weddings is the talk ;
　　Of Isabella's fortune, Mary's shame,
Of Ellen's flight, of Jane's unequal match,
　　And Harry's death, who shot the parson's game.


The sudden rise, the Lord knows how, of some ;
　　The long-expected fall of neighbour Pride ;
The fearful quarrel at the Squire's last night,
　　When scapegrace Edward was his home denied.
The shameful boldness of the envied belle,
　　On whom the maidens look with eyes askance ;
Old Jerry's accident, and Willy's crime,
　　And all the village history and romance.


Of village rights and wrongs they loudly talk,
　　And venture judgments upon all affairs ;
How basely Growl, the lawyer, left his wealth,
　　So basely got, to other than his heirs :
How Grim, the justice, harshly treats the poor,
　　But lets the rich with scarce a touch escape ;
How early Widow Madge put by her weeds,
　　And flaunted in her silk instead of crape.

With broken hints, and solemn shakes of head,

And whispered cautions not to breathe again,

Are secrets told, which none would rest abed

If secrets such good news could long remain.

And aimless slander, gossip vain and void,

And idle talk of little things and great,

Make up the daily business of our life—

Epitome of many a larger state.


And, hearing all, the solemn fountain stands;

No sign or smile disturbs the lion's face;

The fishes in their sculptured beauty rest,

And watch, unmoved, the changes of the place.

And round the basin still the gossips throng,

And tell their hopes and fears, their joys and woes;

And still unheeding all the fountain stands,

Still from the lion's mouth the water flows.

# Invocation.

———◦◦———

Come forth, my love, come with the rising morn.
 Come drain the flower-cups of their virgin dew;
Sweet sleep and pleasant dreams this morning scorn,
 And greet the day that beams so bright for you.
The lark with richest music floods the sky—
 "Come forth, come forth," the burden of his strain;
Resist not, love, th' invoking melody—
 Resist not, love; let *us* not call in vain.


It is the flowery Spring-time: full of life,
 Of gladness, and of joy, all nature is;
The fields with beauteous offerings are rife,
 For beauteous foreheads meet.   Oh, love, for this

Come forth ! the riches waiting thee receive.

What joy with wreath of love-flowers thee to crown,

Thou darling of my heart !   Come, I will weave

    Sweet lays of love to please thee.   Oh, come down !


The blind is drawn, and her fair face I see ;

    Consent smiles on her lips, beams in her eye ;

Her step is on the stair, and joyously

    Her sweet " good morrow" rings.   Oh, blest am I !

And fields, and trees, and flowers, how blest are ye,

    With her dear presence honoured !   All things seem

More rich, more beautiful, more joyous, free,

    Because she smiles on them her smile supreme.


Now she is in the fields ; and rapturously

    All things salute their Queen, and homage pay ;

And from his cloud-concealèd throne on high,

    The lark descends and sings for her his lay ;

The flowers look in her face and brighter grow,

    As seeking to attract her glorious eye ;

The grass is greener where her footsteps go ;

    The trees bow gladly as she passes by.

Now it is Spring-time in the year and heart;
　　And flowers lie thick on earth and on the soul;
A sense of bliss breathes forth from every part,
　　Thrills in each blade, and animates the whole.
But oh, what bliss like ours!   Love shares in all,
　　And has its own which nothing else may share;
Exclusive, all-embracing, free, yet thrall,
　　We walk on earth as though we trod on air.


My beauteous soul, a blessed morning this,
　　As rapt in love we walk among the flowers!
Earth cannot give nor heaven offer bliss
　　To loving hearts, more exquisite than ours.
So for its wealth, the Spring-time we will bless,
　　Bless bird, and flower, and field, and bless the hour
That gives to us this flood of happiness—
　　That gives to us such bliss-receiving power.

# Helen.

A ROMANCE, IN FOUR VERSES.

———◦◦◦———

"Yet was she, certes, but a country lasse ;
Yet she all other country lasses far did passe."

SPENSER.

It is a lowly cottage, of a quaint and antique mien,

With gable end, and straw-thatched roof hid o'er with
mosses green ;

And, standing at its door, is seen a maiden young and fair:

The summer breeze is sporting with the ringlets of her
hair ;

Light auburn is its colour, and its texture like the thread

Which gossamers on sunny days for fairy creatures spread ;

Her eyes are blue and sparkling, and her cheeks are
slightly brown,

Her snowy bosom sweetly peeps above her cotton gown :

For gracefulness of bearing, for a mild yet queenly air,

Few maidens of our lovely land with Helen may compare.

The lane is cool and shaded, overhead the branches meet ;
The birds are singing in the air, the flowers are at the
    feet ;
The leaves are gently rustling, and the insects spread
    their wings ;
The sun is brightly shining, and the lark divinely sings ;
Two happy hearts are throbbing ; one of a maiden fair,
One of a noble stripling, wreathing flow'rets in her hair ;
A blush is on her tear-dewed cheek, her eyes are turned
    away,
As if she feared an upward glance her feelings would
    betray ;
Her lips are partly opened, for a word is trembling there—
And now a murmur musical is floating in the air !

It is an ancient village church, the ivy thickly crawls
Around the mould'ring steeple and the time-decaying walls ;
And now its bells are ringing with a loud and merry peal ;
And loud the village labourers their joyous hearts reveal ;
And youthful village maidens, clad in garments spotless
    white,
Are strewing fragrant flowers, the fair, the beautiful
    and bright ;

And coming from the church's porch four buoyant
  forms are seen ;
The two are peerless creatures in their dress of snowy
  sheen,
And two are fair and noble youths : the one, with
  conscious pride,
Supports a blushing maiden, and young Helen is a bride.


It is a noble mansion where re-echo joyous sounds,
For through the high and stately pile festivity abounds ;
From every window splendour gleams, the trees with
  lamps are hung,
And men's and women's voices sweetly blend in choral
  song ;
The lordly and the lowly are in happy concord seen,
Now laughing at some rustic joke, now dancing on the
  green ;
The spacious rooms are crowded with the manly and
  the fair,
And hopeful hearts, and sparkling eyes, and merry lips
  are there :
But far above them all appears, in beauty and in grace,
The lowly village maiden, now the mistress of the place.

# The Poet's Heritage.

———✦———

From my little dingy office—
A little dingy room—
Oh, my spirit freely wanders
'Mid flowers and perfume :
With a merry heart and buoyant,
I scent the coming breeze,
As it ruffles o'er the streamlet
And murmurs through the trees.


Through the thickly coated window
The sun can scarcely peep ;
Yet I feel his glowing splendour,
And gambol with the sheep ;

With an ecstasy of rapture,
　My soul expands her wings,
For the bee is gaily booming—
　The lark in glory sings.


There the fairy forms romantic
　Of poet's gladsome lay,
In their dances wild and antic,
　Upon the greensward play :
There in every tree's a Dryad ;
　And, skipping o'er the lawn,
In its light and bounding movement,
　Is seen the graceful fawn.


While in fancy far I ramble
　Through field, and lane, and dell—
While the choristers of nature
　Their joyance loudly tell—
What to me is Fortune's frowning ?
　What rank or state to me ?
I can own the whole creation,
　And live content and free !

See the heavens rich in glory—
  The mountain's snow-capped shrine—
See the boundlessness of ocean :
  Sky, mountain, sea, are mine !
Whence, despite life's care and canker,
  Do I rich tribute claim ;
All this wealth's for my possessing,
  On all I stamp my name !

# On the Inauguration

OF

# The Attwood Statue at Birmingham,

JUNE 7TH, 1859.

———◇———

THIS day a noble work is done,

A people's gratitude by merit won

Comes sweetly on the wings of time,

With fragrancy, and pleasant odours rife.

And 'neath the over-arching, blue, sublime,

Unclouded heavens, in their thousands meet,

The sons of those who fought for freedom and for
life,

And won, though serried ranks of might had sworn to
their defeat.

This day a noble work was done.

Beneath the brightest summer's sun

The monument of gratitude was raised :

He whom a people loved, a people praised ;

And as upon that noble face they gazed,

Arose the shout, and rung the goodly cheer,

Which told that still the patriot work is prized, the patriot
    dear.


Oh, fitting day for such a worthy deed !

The day on which he saw his work succeed :

The day when years long past, confiding and serene,

The Monarch set his seal to Freedom's act :

The day which men praise God for having seen :

The day when, for a time, the long-stretched bow was
    slacked,

That for a freer shot, a nobler aim,

It might again be bent, and win an equal fame.


That day is ours.   The children we

For whom this noble one, and his compeers,

With self-forgetfulness, and bravely free

From evil passions filling slaves with fears,

Pursued their onward march from field to field
Of moral conquest, and unsullied victory.
They made the stubborn and opposing phalanx yield;
And bow'd a lordly few into a people's will.
No blood is on the laurels which they won.
Their deeds the angels e'en might smile upon.
Oh, may their godlike spirit be among us still!


The memory of noble men's the sweetest thing
That blesses earth.   From it will ever spring
The best incentives prompting glorious deeds.
Life's roses they unchoked with noisome weeds.
Their fragrance is eternal; and we feel,
Inhaling joyously their rich perfume,
How holy is the Power which thus can seal
A mortal action with perennial bloom.
Such, ATTWOOD, was thy life; and such to-day
The thoughts which fire us while our gratitude we
    pay.


Oh, noble was the work he wrought!
He filled a land with Freedom's fire;
And made the lowliest aspire.

His words, with wisest counsel fraught,
Were heard till all their spirit caught!
And myriads, though moved and swayed
By fiery zeal, his voice obeyed,
And Order, Peace, and Law in every art displayed.


A people giant-like in banded might;
A people godlike in their use of power;
Unswerving lovers of the true and right;
With love of Liberty their richest dower.
How well they answered to their leader's voice,
And made the wise, and brave, and good rejoice,
That worthy of their ancient fame were they;
That not in vain had Cromwell drawn his sword;
And not in vain had Milton penned his mightier
    word,
That none henceforth should chains upon his England
    lay.


O men for whom he toiled, and fought, and won,
Remember him through ages still to run.
Unto your children as a legacy bequeathe
The record of the work he did, ere smiling death,

When crowned with honours and with blessings, called
The patriot to his reward ; and unappalled
He heard the summons ; for he knew
Pure motives had inspired the work he lived to do.

O men, the children of a dauntless race,
Look on him moulded here ; look on him face to face.
The very lineaments of him are here.
His living fire still animates the stone.
Thanks to the artist's skill, you now may know
The man whose work was for his country's good alone.
And look on him your fathers honoured so.
Oh prove your worth !  Still honour him, and crown the
    name
Of ATTWOOD with a grateful people's never-ending fame.

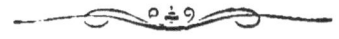

# The Queen of Beauty.

———◆———

THE summer eve was bright and cool;
   The fields were strewn with hay;
The rushes whistled on the pool;
   The moths began to play;
And thou and I the garden throng h
   Went rambling hand in hand;
And sweeter breezes never blew
   Than those our foreheads fanned.


The roses clustered round the wall;
   The white rose and the red;
O'er thee, the loveliest rose of all,
   A bower of roses spread.

Beneath their rich and fragrant shade
 We lingered fancy-free ;
And every rose for beauty paid
 Its tribute unto thee.


Then slowly round the pool we strayed,
 And wooed the sunny breeze ;
The ripples watched the waters made,
 Kissed by o'er-arching trees.
Though all was summer beauty there,
 In richness and in grace,
The waves reflected nought so fair,
 So lovely, as thy face.


The setting sun ; the illumined sky ;
 The clouds of brightest hue ;
The gorgeous jewelled dragon-fly ;
 The birds that round us flew ;
The damask-tinted leaves above,
 All did their tribute bear ;
But thou, O Lizzie, reigned my love,
 The Queen of Beauty there.

# Summer Time.

Oh, pleasant 'tis in Summer time
 Beneath the trees to lie ;
Far-spreading beech, or odorous lime,
 Or broad oak tow'ring high.
To dream, and dream the hours away,
 In indolent delight ;
To dream such dreams as never play
 About the brain at night.


For fancy then is uncontrolled,
 Not bound in chains of sleep ;
Can freer, broader wings unfold,
 And take a wider sweep.

Wherever beauty is can build
  A nest to harbour in;
And common things with glory gild,
  And joy from all things win.


On earth, in air, through sea and sky,
  Will glorious visions raise;
The light, white clouds that dove-like fly,
  And pass you as you gaze.
A thousand lovely things are made
  By Fancy's dreamy power,
But true and real as yonder blade,
  Or bee upon the flower.


And scarce asleep, nor scarce awake,
  The world with music full,
Sweet murmurs on the senses break,
  Which still the senses lull.
No pain of thought, for thought is not—
  Serene, and calm, and still,
Light summer clouds of fancies float
  Around you as they will.

The past comes gently to the mind,
   Its sunny hours alone ;
The present bright, solacing, kind,
   With joyous pictures strown.
The future, gracious as a bride,
   Upon your vision beams,
No cloud or darkness there to hide
   The splendour of your dreams.


O Summer time ! sweet Summer time !
   Beneath the trees to lie,
Far-spreading beach, or odorous lime,
   Or broad oak tow'ring high.
To dream, and dream the hours away,
   In indolent delight ;
To dream such dreams as never play
   About the brain at night.

# Solferino.

———◆◇◆———

FULL brightly in the Italian sky
  The sun hangs over field and plain,
  And vine and olive, maize and grain,
Of plenty tell the harvest nigh.

The birds fly on in love's delight,
  And sing their songs with boundless glee ;
  And men and maidens merrily
Their voices with the strains unite.

For visions of a happier time,
  Of Freedom's bright and glorious reign,
  Sustained the land to bear the pain
Of war's sublime, or bloody crime.

And swiftly o'er the landscape came
   The thunder-roll of cannon's voice ;
   And loud the tumult and the noise
Which told the approach of fire and flame.

The dun clouds rise, and shame the sky ;
   The sun is hid in rolling smoke,
   And sulphurous mists the senses choke,
And Death is smiling hideously.

With shock on shock of murderous force,
   Contending armies clash and meet ;
   And streams of blood o'erflow the feet ;
And man is trampled on by horse.

In wild confusion, cries, and groans,
   The work of death goes fiercely on ;
   And triumph and defeat are won
On either side : pale Fury owns

She ne'er beheld a scene so sad—
   What bitter wrongs to prompt such deeds ;
   What awful hate to win such meeds ;
The sight might make the calmest mad.

From dawn till night o'erhung the sky,
   The death-increasing carnage reigns ;
   And red on Solferino's plains,
The dead and dying mingled lie.

And all for nought—oh, veil the eyes,
   And let the tears in silence flow !
   Oh, weep for such a scene of woe ;
And pray a brighter future rise !

# In Memoriam.

## I.

### Joseph Sturge.

Mourn all who noble deeds admire ;
   Mourn all who noble lives revere ;
   His worth will consecrate the tear :
His life a spark of Love's true fire.

His love was wide as grief and woe ;
   His heart as large as sorrow's reign ;
   His hand brought solace where was pain ;
His charity to all did flow.

Unchecked by race, or clime, or creed :
   O'er every land his mercy ran :
   His sympathies were for the man :
His grace where'er was wrong, or need.

For slaves redeemed his love reveal :

  And orphans, fathered, bless his name ;

  And outcasts' tears enrich his fame ;

And widows' prayers his glory seal.


Like fragrant roses through his life,

  His deeds are scattered fair and sweet :

  His garland is for heaven meet :

With Christian works his years were rife.


Rejoice, that such have lived on earth :

  Rejoice, that such are with us still :

  But purer heart, serener will,

Ne'er graced a man with Christian worth,


Than his whose loss we mourn to-day :

  But mourn with mingled joy and woe—

  Joy that his life such deeds did show ;

Woe that such worth is ta'en away.


His glory is the poor man's praise ;

  His fame, the blessings of the poor ;

  His memory will e'er endure,

While truth and goodness love can raise.

His life devout, calm, joyous, brave :
   His name enshrined in purest love :
   His soul is with the blest above :
And holy tears make green his grave.

True friend of man, 'tis vain to urge
   Thy greatness, known to all so well ;
   But ever will the memory dwell
With fondness on the name of STURGE.

*May* 20*th*, 1859.

# In Memoriam.

## II.

### David Cox.

Dear child of nature, lover of the hills,

Of sunny downs, of wild, uncultured plains,

Where fragrant gorse, or sparkling heather fills

The eye with wonder and delight; and pleasure reigns

Unfettered; free as is the lark, whose strains

Are fitting music for such glorious haunts.—

No more thy genius-guided hand will trace

The spots we love; no more from place to place

By thy rich, wonder-working fancy led,

Shall we each well-remembered scene retread.

Reft of its skill thy hand all powerless lies;

Reft of their fire are thy far-seeing eyes;

But thy creations live : Death vainly vaunts :

*They* immortality upon thee shed.

# The Moss-Rose.

SENT IN A LETTER FROM DEVONSHIRE.

———◦———

### 1.

Of all the flowers the Summer brings,
   The Moss-Rose is the sweetest;
For fragrance o'er its beauty flings
   Of graces the completest.
Of Flora's realm it is the queen,
   Arrayed in Eastern splendour;
And, oh, despite its regal mien,
   The flower of lovers tender.

### 2.

But sweeter than the sweetest rose
  In England's gardens growing,
The one that now before me glows,
  Its beauty joy-bestowing ;
For brightest eyes have o'er it hung ;
  'Twas plucked by loving fingers :
And all the grace love round it flung,
  Still on its petals lingers.

### 3.

A charm is ever on the flower
  Love's dimpling finger presses ;
And fresh as in its native bower,
  It bears the dear caresses.
And unto me this Rose will bloom,
  The purest bliss conveying,
Escaping still the common doom,
  'Twill never know decaying.

## The Roe.

FROM THE GERMAN OF UHLAND.

———◦—◦———

Through fields and woods at early dawn,
    A hunter chased a roe,
When through a garden-hedge he saw
    A rosy maiden glow.

What to the good steed has befall'n?
    Or has he lost his way?
What to the worthy hunter's chanced,
    No more to hunt his prey?

Yet swiftly over hill and dale,
    Still flees the anxious roe;
Rest, silly thing! the hunter has
    Forgot thee long ago!

# The Serenade.*

FROM THE GERMAN OF UHLAND.

———◆◇◆———

" WHAT wakens me from slumber now,
　　With music's sweetest power ?
O mother, see who it may be,
　　At such an early hour."

" I nothing see ; I nothing hear.
　　O, slumber on so mild :
No serenade is brought thee now,
　　My poor—my sickly child ! "

" It is not music of the earth,
　　That thrills me with its might,
But angels call my soul with song :
　　So, mother, now, good night."

---

* This version of Uhland's delightful " Serenade " has been set
to exquisite music by my friend Mr. Thomas Anderton, a com-
poser to whose genius the lovers of music will ere long be
grateful.

# To You.

FROM THE GERMAN OF UHLAND.

THINE eyes are not the heaven's blue,
Thy cheeks have not the rose's hue,
　　Nor lilies are thy arms and breast :
O, what a glorious Spring it were,
If flowery hill and valley fair,
　　Were with such roses, lilies, blest !
And to the all-embracing heaven,
The clear blue of thine eyes were given.

# Poesy.

## FROM THE GERMAN OF GOETHE.

———◆———

His rude rough children here God sent,
   Sent Science, Order, Law, and Art,
   Did heaven's grace to them impart,
The earth's sad loss to supplement.

Naked from heaven here they came,
   And nought of meet behaviour knew ;
   But Poesy her garments threw
Around them, and they had not shame.

London : Printed by SMITH, ELDER and Co., Little Green Arbour Court, L.C

BY THE SAME AUTHOR,

# THE LAMP OF LIFE.

*Foolscap 8vo.* 5s.

## OPINIONS OF THE PRESS.

### LITERARY GAZETTE.

" Had this poem borne on its title-page some well-known name, it might have been received with popular favour. . . . .

" These descriptive passages are written with spirit; but the chief merit of the poem lies in the sustained narrative of inward thoughts and feelings, partly in the same track as Newman's *Phases of Faith*, but leading at last to a Rock of Faith instead of the Slough of Despond, where that book leaves its readers."

### TAIT'S MAGAZINE.

" In clumps of pretty verses, not long, but often sweet and full of quaint thoughtfulness, this writer records nearly all that he perhaps remembers of his own heart struggles. . . We should not have run out so long our notice of this little volume if we had not experienced much pleasure in its perusal. It is in construction, plot and style, out of the common walk; and our readers see that what the writer had to say he has told well."

### WEEKLY DISPATCH.

" This is a semi-religious poem of great beauty of utterance, exquisite rhythm, lofty, though not vivid imagery, and of a didactic order of construction. Its aspirations, which lift great earthly deeds, and still greater human thoughts, heavenwards, are conceived in a true poet-spirit, and, as an example of continued soliloquy, mingling exultation and wailing together, it is a work of no common order."

### BIRMINGHAM JOURNAL.

" We recommend this well-written history—a life of trouble and doubt, ending in firm faith in Christianity and deep religious feeling—to those, and those only, who can sympathise with the struggles and fears of a contemplative and earnest soul, or those who can appreciate a poem of calm and flowing melody and much descriptive power."

# OPINIONS OF THE PRESS.

## THE LEADER.

" He has tenderness and grace, and seems to speak out of his own veritable strugglings for what he conceives to be genuine holiness."

## ECLECTIC REVIEW.

" The book delineates, in a series of short poems, the history of a mind of the reflective and speculative order, which, however, has never entirely lost its faith in the existence and love of God, and is, therefore, open to the means of relief which prayer presents. The aid and illumination eventually realized give a happy tone to many of the poems, and leave a pleasant effect on the reader's mind. Much of the versification is good, and the author displays considerable power of depicting those moods of mind which are incident to temperaments of his class."

## THE BRISTOL ADVERTISER.

" This anonymous poem has pleased us very much. It is not grand, brilliant, or great, and that is why we like it. There is nothing mad, melodramatic, or spasmodic about it. It is sober, simple, sweet, generally musical, true to the heart, and true to God. It is religious without being wild, and human without being silly. There is scarcely a Latin word from beginning to end. Our good old mother Saxon reigns through all these 220 pages of genuine and easy versification. The subject is the old, the everlasting one. The struggles of a honest mind with doubt : the thirst for God ; the redeeming ecstacies of love ; the immortal mystery of death ; the agonies of prayer ; the dawn of faith ; the fervid sympathies and loyalties of patriotism, arising out of and flowing into the religious life ; and, at last, the serene and sacred enjoyment of Christ's beautiful faith—such are the experiences of the author and the themes of his book."

## LIVERPOOL DAILY POST.

" There is simple truth and nature, a loving charm about them, which, as far as we know, are unexampled and unsurpassed. They might be called 'Lyrics of Home.' "

## NORTH DEVON JOURNAL.

" This strangely interesting work presents all the charms of vivid impressions accurately noted down as they occurred, and which, with pleasing ingenuity, the author has formed into a ' Poem of Life,' and song of the soul perfectly unique in its kind."

LONDON : SIMPKIN, MARSHALL AND CO.

ALSO, BY THE SAME AUTHOR,

# POEMS OF THE FIELDS AND THE TOWN.

*Small 8vo.*   5s.

## OPINIONS OF THE PRESS.

### GLOBE.

"This little volume is dedicated with a brotherly feeling 'to Edward Capern, rural postman and poet,' and appears to be the produce of a congenial mind. Mr. Langford's feeling for the beauties of nature is sincere, his sense of the domestic affections pure and fervent, and he expresses both in language sufficiently flowing. His meaning is always transparent, his words seem to rise naturally to the subject, not to be dragged from the ends of the earth to 'darken counsel.' In the 'Death-bed of Alfred' we have an insight into the writer's higher moods; and in 'My Riches' he not only reveals his own simple sources of enjoyment, but suggests that they lie open about our own path. The Chevalier de Chatelain has selected several of these poems for translation, and one, peculiarly pleasing, by the wife of the author, appears both in its English and French dress."

### WEEKLY DISPATCH.

"Some of the love lyrics are exquisite, and in their expression are commendably within the limits of true taste and right feeling. We wish the volume a wide circulation and every success."

### LITERARY GAZETTE.

"A pious tone breathes through the entire collection, and home feelings and domestic joys are described with considerable though quiet power. 'To my Wife,' and 'When will the Letter come' we like much. * * * We are continually seeing far more pretentious volumes of verse, the quality of which is greatly inferior to that of Mr. Langford."

### COVENTRY HERALD.

"It is just the thing to read this brilliant July weather; for any one of poetic temperament who has plenty of time to spare to loll about in the shades of green trees, it would be an invaluable pocket companion. * * * All his utterances are pure in expression and utterly unexceptionable in point of sentiment."

## LONDON: SIMPKIN, MARSHALL AND CO.

IN LOVING MEMORY OF

# JOHN ALFRED LANGFORD,

WHO DIED JANUARY 24th, 1903.

AGED 79.

—

INTERRED AT GENERAL CEMETERY JANUARY 28TH, 1903

85, FERNLEY ROAD,
SPARKHILL

# CROSSING THE BAR.

Sunset and evening star,
   And one clear call for me !
And may there be no moaning of the bar,
   When I put out to sea,

But such a tide as moving seems asleep,
   Too full for sound or foam,
When that which drew from out the boundless deep
   Turns again home.

Twilight and evening bell,
   And after that the dark !
And may there be no sadness of farewell,
   When I embark.

For tho' from out our bourne of time and place
   The flood may bear me far,
I hope to meet my Pilot face to face
   When I have crossed the bar.

*Tennyson.*

www.ingramcontent.com/pod-product-compliance
Lightning Source LLC
Chambersburg PA
CBHW021108020726
47500CB00003B/655